CW00622012

# NORTHERN STORIES
## Volume Three

# NORTHERN STORIES
## Volume Three

*Edited by Berlie Doherty and Stanley Middleton*

LITTLEWOOD ARC
1992

ISBN 0 946407 85 1

Published by Littlewood Arc, The Nanholme Centre,
Shaw Wood Road, Todmorden, Lancashire OL14 6DA
Design and Print by Arc & Throstle Press, Todmorden
Typeset by Lasertext Ltd., Stretford, Manchester

The publishers acknowledge financial assistance from Yorkshire and Humberside Arts Board and North West Arts Board.

# CONTENTS

## PREFACE

To read a short story is to pause for a moment at the lighted window of a room in a strange house, understanding at once the relationship that exists between the people in the room, and what has led up to this moment, and moving on. At its best it will ensure that the slightest movements and expressions of those people will remain with you. Here short does not mean slight or condensed but fleeting, a captured moment.

The short story is a jewel of an art form, and the readers of this collection will find a string of jewels here, each with its own intensity and richness.

*Berlie Doherty*

The power of a short story is determined not only by its shape, but by choice of incidental detail. One cannot afford to include a phrase which might allow the reader's attention to wander off-track. This means constant revision and questioning by the writer. Once this principle is grasped then one can occasionally break the rule, but not often. Don't forget Chekhov's gun hanging on the wall. Once one has mentioned it, it must be fired before the story ends. But make it all look inevitable and easy.

*Stanley Middleton*

## Margaret Lesser

*Voices*

I am coming – no, I come – from Leipzig. Excuse my first mistake. Usually I am satisfactory or even excellent, they say so at school. I come from Leipzig and in the summer of the year 1992 I have come to Manchester to stay with my exchange-friend Peter, who is also a boy of fourteen.

If only I had not!

Please do not misunderstand – I have always been a fan of England, all my life. Charles Dickens, fish-and-chips, Manchester United. Also Tower of London, Scottish Highlands and Hallelujah Chorus. – This chorus is in fact by Händel, a man from Halle in Germany, but they have explained in my school (which is the St Thomas' Choir School of Leipzig, you may have heard of it) that Händel now counts as an Englishman and has definitively lost his umlaut. – It was my great wish to go to England. My mother too was pleased. I have no father.

Peter also. This I think is why they coupled us together. Peter and me, we have the fatherlessness in common. Otherwise we are not so similar. He is an only child. I am the elder brother of four dumb sisters. No, they are not dumb in English; they twitter continuously. They are however not earnest, they are too young. We are poor – extra poor on account of the Glorious Unification. (I forgot to say: I am also a big fan of the English irony.) Peter's family, on the other hand, is very rich. They live, at least, in a house with many rooms and a garden – Peter, his mother and a large ginger tomcat.

Peter's mother drove us home from Manchester Airport along winding lanes between fields of wheat. Peter said: "Trust you, Mum! Why don't you use the motorway?"

She said: "I thought Christoph might like to see a little of the Cheshire countryside, it's so . . . "

"Christ!" he said. I have not so far mentioned that he has already a baritone voice, with whiskers. I, on the other hand, am still an alto (though now in my last days). About this I have no complexes at all. In the time of Johann Sebastian Bach it was common for boys to remain altos until their eighteenth year. In the Choir School, they have told me, I am quite convenient.

We drove past groups of black-and-white cows – a pair of horses, nose to nose, kissing maybe – a stream with a little bridge like a child's toy – many rich green trees. Then the houses began – I would say stout, square burghers' houses – and then a few shops.

"You'll help me carry some stuff from the supermarket, won't you?" said Peter's mother, turning round in the driver's seat.

"What do you think the trolleys are for!" said Peter.

I was not sure what to do, but I went with her into the shop. "What would you like for supper?" she said. "You choose." She smiled upward when she said this, since even beside me she is a very small woman, very pale in the hair and also the face. I chose vegetarian hot dogs (because, like Cheshire, I am whenever possible green), potato nuggets (these are perhaps typically English), sauerkraut (a reminder of Germany), and much chocolate ice cream. It is my experience that everybody, however mature, likes chocolate ice cream. Peter's mother said only "Yes" and "That's a good idea!" when I made each selection. Otherwise she was quiet, pensive, with hesitant hands.

We drove on. The shops changed to a row of dolls' houses climbing up a hill. Little doors with bright brass knobs and tiara-windows on their heads. Little flights of steps up to the front doors, many flowers growing on the walls and round the windows. In the sky above, a line of chimneys also marching up the hill, like soldiers. In Germany we do not have so many chimneys.

At the top of the hill the street opened up to make a square, with a big church and two pubs. And then came our house, Peter's house.

"Take Christoph to his room, love," said Peter's mother. "Why don't you two get to know each other while he unpacks and I make supper?" Her voice is breathy, it fades away at the end of sentences. As we singers say, she has no support. "Yes?" she said, looking at Peter.

"Come on then!" he said, grabbing both my cases. "If we get a move on we'll be finished with all this in time to watch Clive James."

Up and up we climbed. A narrow staircase with strange, unreasonable side-passages leading off it from time to time. "Here," he said. "You want anything, you just shout. You don't want to talk, do you? I mean, what about?"

Through the window, as I hung up my clothes, I could see a toy village far below. Interlocking garden plots, a garage stuck in among the jumble, the back of the church, a flag (red cross on white) fluttering from its tower. In a nearby garden the upturned rump and dimpled knee-backs of a woman weeding. Further away, two children passionately embracing a collie. The ginger tomcat striding across his lawn.

Over supper in the kitchen Peter's mother made suggestions. "I expect Christoph would like to see the centre of Manchester," she said. "Do you like pictures, Christoph? Perhaps the Whitworth, or the City Art Gallery...? Or – here's an idea – there's a reproduction of a milltown-street somewhere... Or are you more interested in Science and Industry, Christoph...?"

Peter said nothing until a certain moment, when he looked at his watch and said, "Mind if we go now, Mum? – Clive James."

"Of course," said his mother. "If that's what Christoph..." Her voice as usual faded away. She began to pile up the chocolate ice cream plates. Always with hesitant, I would say almost trembling, hands.

On the next day a classmate of Peter's arrived with a whole set of new computer games. It is well known that more than two people cannot conveniently sit in front of one computer screen.

Peter's mother said: "I don't suppose, Christoph..." and hung down her head. We were washing up in the kitchen. I was drying. This, I am freely admitting, I do not often do in my own house in Leipzig.

"I don't suppose you'd like to come with me and pick blackberries?"

"Blackberries?"

"Only once they're ripe, they're so quickly gone," she said hastily, anxious in the eyes, pink in the cheeks. "I know it's a childish idea."

"I only wish to ask: what are blackberries?"

We searched in a dictionary, and I understood.

"You mustn't mind if Peter's a bit full of himself," she said, as we picked our way through the brambles in the churchyard. (For it is in the churchyards that blackberries are growing in England, and thus the bodies of the dead feed the fruit of the living. I am a big fan of this typically English concept.)

"He's going through a phase, is Peter," said his mother, licking the blood from her fingers. "It's not his fault."

The ginger tomcat stalked magnificently past, with his eye on the blackbirds.

"He's clever, you see," said Peter's mother anxiously, "and I'm not. That's how he got a scholarship to this famous school he's at. Peter's father was clever. When he went, he left us the house and his brains – in Peter's head. I shouldn't be surprised if you were clever too," she added politely. "And I know you're musical as well! That's nice, isn't it? There's always room at a party for someone who can sit down at a piano and start a sing-song. I've always wanted to play myself."

"What would you like to play?"

"Oh, nice tunes. You know. Any nice tunes. But there wasn't the money for it. And I dare say I shouldn't have been clever enough."

"I could teach you something," I said. In the house there was a piano – horribly out of tune, but with most of the notes still operating.

"Thanks all the same," she said, "but it's a bit late for me. You just have a good time with Peter. That's what you're here for."

On the next day it transpired that Peter was having to work urgently on a history project. In England, he explained to me, it is necessary to produce these written projects at two-week intervals throughout the year, winter and summer, term-time and holiday-time. Already he was behind with this task and must immediately shut himself up in his room and work night and day. If I heard his electric guitar, this was only because he needed it to stimulate his intellect.

So in the afternoon his mother and I went into the centre of Manchester to see a film called Fantasia. "It's just your kind of thing," she said. "Full of classical music and that. And I love going to the cinema in the afternoon, don't you? Reminds me of skiving off school. – I shouldn't say that to a boy your age. Silly me."

In the dark she passed me a bag of crisps. "I'll tell you something," she whispered. "This is my birthday treat. I'm thirty-one today, isn't it dreaful! Peter's father's forty-five, and goodness knows what he looks like now. Good-looking, he used to be – you can see it in Peter, can't you? That's another thing he has to cope with: he's too good-looking. It's difficult for a boy."

This difficulty, at least, I do not suffer from.

When we returned home Peter was not there. "He'll have gone into Altrincham," said his mother, "to see some of his mates. A boy can't be working *all* the time." We made tea and took it out into the garden, which was warm, closed-in, like a greenhouse. Like the greenhouse in the Wagner song, I said to Peter's mother, but she had not heard of this composer or the *Wesendoncklieder*. These too I could one day introduce to her, also *Tristan*.

"Cheshire weather," said Peter's mother. "You'll see: after a whole day like this, suddenly in the evening the sky will clear, and the sun will shine quite different, and there'll be a fresh little breeze that lifts your heart up. Only you have to suffer for it first."

I ate silently Marmite sandwiches and more scones.

"Gives me terrible headaches," she said. "You wouldn't believe. Like the tortures of the – what's the word?"

"The Stasi?"

"I was thinking of the Inquisition. But it's all right now. You've heard of Wilbur Lang, I expect."

"No."

"No? Oh well, I suppose Leipzig's a bit out of the way. He's a man with powers."

She looked at me with the eyes of my youngest sister when she wishes me to agree that fairies do exist.

"Powers?"

"He only has to rest his hands... Right inside you, he sees right inside you at the first glance. Knows what your illness is, your past, your future..."

"You should see first a medical doctor!" I cried.

"I shall be all right now..."

"This is dangerous!"

"You're a nice boy," she said, "thoughtful. But you don't need to worry your head, I know a man with powers when I see one. – Where's this son of mine!"

It was as she said. By seven o'clock the passion had cleared out of the air, and the garden, the pink roses, the sky, were as light and sane as Mozart.

"I've got a plan for you two boys," said Peter's mother to me. "For tomorrow evening. In the morning I'll be cleaning for my ladies as usual, of course – not to speak of old Mr Mellon, with his dogs. But in the afternoon I'm going to make all your favourite food – well Peter's favourite food, but I hope you'll like it too. Roast turkey with all the trimmings, just like Christmas, and a choice of trifle or apple pie and cream. It's a bit hot for pudding, I think, don't you?"

"Yes," I said.

"And I'll invite round all the old friends and the family to meet Peter's nice German friend. His Nana – he's always been fond of his Nana, ever since he was a baby. And old George, that used to take him for walks in the park after his father left. And my sister Sharon – she'll come over from Liverpool with her boys, I know she will. And we'll have a great time, like in the old days."

She was excited like a girl. "I too!" I said.

"What?"

"I too will have a great time."

It grew at last cold, and we went into the house. The telephone rang.

"Oh, I see..." said Peter's mother. "Well, we were wondering. Oh, I see."

"He's staying the night with a friend," she explained. "A real expert on the history Peter's writing about. Masses of reference books. You can't argue with the complete Cambridge Modern History, can you? He'll be back tomorrow."

Tomorrow was for us a day of gala, of heroic endeavour. At midday Peter's mother returned from her cleaning jobs and straight away we hurried to the kitchen. Chopping, mixing, stuffing. Basting, turning, setting potatoes under the meat.

"Why don't you play to me?" she said. "I appreciate your help, but seeing you can play the piano... Make a nice background."

The friends and relations had been summoned and had all been fortunately free. She was happy.

On the hideous piano I was playing, in uninterrupted stream, preludes and fugues, a Brahms rhapsody, nocturnes and ballades by Chopin.

It was evening. Peter came in, a little hot, a little red. His mother, now in a clean dress ready for entertaining, told him what was to be expected.

"What?" he said.

"I thought you'd like it – so your friend can see an English Christmas – "

"In July?"

"And all the old friends – "

"Well, you might have asked me beforehand. You might just have consulted me. It might just have been a good idea."

"Peter..."

"Because as a matter of fact I've got to go out again."

"Now?"

"Can't you see them waiting for me outside?"

Through the window it was indeed possible to see a car waiting with its engine running. Several grinning boys inside.

"Couldn't you..."

"Don't be sillier than you can help," he said, and laughed.

Then it was that the first bad thing – oh God oh God oh God – happened. I hit him full across the face with the back of my left hand.

He laughed again, and left.

Then it was that the second bad thing – oh God oh God oh God oh God – happened. I took in my hands the face of his mother and into her lips I placed a kiss.

## Simon Gotts

### *The Cedar of Lebanon*

Nurse de la Mare says I can't get up till tomorrow, because I told her my stitches hurt. "Are they paining you?" she says. She has a funny way of talking sometimes. She has dark hair and dark eyes and I can't decide if maybe she is foreign too, not just her husband. The first time I told her I wanted to spend a penny, she thought I wanted to buy something. Now she fetches one of the bottles, like the ones they have in the labs at school. When I have finished she holds it up and looks at it swishing about, all golden, and says that I should give it its proper name at my age.

"If they're paining you, I'll get you something to ease them. Do they itch?" Her eyes are big and shiny. They make mine want to water, because they are so kind. I nod my head and she goes off to find some stuff to make the stitches feel better. The window is open and the curtains flap in the breeze. There is a wood pigeon who has come every evening this week, to sit on the branch of the tree outside the window behind Jerry's bed and say "cru, cru", over and over until Jerry and Roger and I all fall asleep. We've never seen him, because the window is too small and square and he always hides in the branches. Tomorrow, when I can get up, I'll be able to see him and I'll tell Jerry and Roger what he looks like, whether he is old and scraggy, or young and sleek. Then we'll have a competition to think of a name for him. I asked Nurse de la Mare to look for him but she couldn't see him, she said. But she told me the name of the tree. The Cedar of Lebanon. She said it was a hundred years old and would still be here in another hundred years, when we were all gone.

I think about the country where the tree comes from, which is hot and sandy probably. The sun shines through the branches of The Cedar of Lebanon into my eyes and when I close them it is like being there, in Lebanon, and instead of Roger and Jerry there are Arabs all round me, roasting a sheep over their brush wood fires and singing in soft, droning voices.

I woke up and found I had missed my supper. They didn't bother to see if I wanted any. At first I forgot where I was and started to get out of bed, then I felt dizzy. One of the porters let go of the trolley he was wheeling down the aisle and lifted my feet back in the bed again.

"Alright, Mr Grice, you just have a bit more of a rest, and I'll find you some grub in a minute," he said.

He hurried off down the aisle, getting smaller and smaller, then disappeared through the double doors with the portholes in them. I try to think how long have I been here. Surely not more than a few days? Maybe they've forgotten me. I call out as loud as I can for the nurse.

A nurse in a light blue uniform appears through the double doors with the portholes and squeaks towards me along the linoleum. It is not Nurse de la Mare. I start to ask her how long I have been here, but she ignores me and squeaks straight past me and through the other double doors, which have square windows, not portholes. High up, behind my head, the wood pigeon starts up, "cru, cru," sitting in the tree outside the window, which I can't see. I wanted to face the window, but they have given me a bed which only looks onto a lot of other beds, with sick-faced men in them, and behind them a grey wall with pink bits where the paint has peeled. I turn round to try to see the window and the porter appears at the side of me.

"Alright, Mr Grice, patience, patience," he says. He swings a tray on a stand over the bed and reaches down onto the bottom of his trolley for a bowl of porridge. "I think you can manage that, can't you?" he says, looking on his trolley for a spoon.

I tell him that I don't like porridge; we're supposed to have a biscuit and a glass of milk for supper, but he isn't listening. He wheels his trolley off again, down the aisle, out of the square window doors. I was going to ask him how long I have been here, but it's too late. I close my eyes and try to remember where I was yesterday.

When I taste the porridge it is stone cold, and lumpy, like sick. The ward is dark and I realise that the porter has forgotten me. Someone has also forgotten to turn the night lights on. I remember Nurse de la Mare coming round once when the night lights were on, and looking at us while we were asleep, except that I was only pretending, because of my stitches and the heat. Though the window was still open the night lights made the room seem more stuffy and hot than it was during the day. I remember how she looked at us each in turn, Roger, me, then Jerry. She stayed next to Jerry's bed for a long time, then she reached out and I saw her touching his head. I could hear her making a little "cru cru" sound like a pigeon, as she moved her fingers through his damp, curly hair. Eventually she stopped stroking him and walked past me out of the room, with a swish of cool air. I breathed in and held till I couldn't hold it any more. All I wished was that it had been dark, so that I would not have seen her stroking him like that, with her pale, fluttering fingertips.

***

I open my eyes and the clock says half past six, which is breakfast time in hospital. Nurse Craig, the negro lady, brings round the cornflakes and she makes me laugh, though I'm a little afraid of her, because my family does not know any negro people. She pours the milk on with a ladle from a big metal drum, like the Beadle in Oliver Twist, which is the book I am reading at present. There are inky black pictures of all the important scenes, and my favourite is the bit where Bill Sykes hangs himself off the roof, which I have skipped ahead and read already. I show Nurse Craig the picture of the Beadle and she opens her mouth wide and laughs. She has a tongue so fat, pink and soft that it looks as though it would make a really comfortable bed to curl up on. Roger is having his breakfast too, but Jerry doesn't want any. He says he just wants to sleep. Nurse Craig tries to sit him up but he is too grumpy and he hits her big fat arm with his little fist. She takes it away quickly as if she has been stung by a bee. She looks at me and shakes her head and clucks her tongue.

"You tell him Peter. You' the oldest, I shall rely on you to talk some sense into that boy."

When Nurse Craig has gone, Roger leans over from his bed, using his plastered leg to balance his body, and pulls Jerry's hair. Jerry can't be bothered to hit him, he just hides his head further under the blankets. I haven't seen him eat anything for at least two days and it makes me unhappy to think about it.

I know I'm not supposed to get up, because I haven't been told yet by Nurse de la Mare, but I don't see what harm it will do. So I pull back my blankets and lower my feet very carefully to the floor. The lino is so cool after the sweaty bed that it makes me want to sing and dance. I slide over to Jerry's bed, keeping my feet on the lino all the way, to make the most of it. Nurse Craig has opened the window and I can feel the air from outside hotting up already for another boiling, sunny day. Jerry is deep down under the blankets. He must be suffocating down there. I sit down on his bed and open his locker. In it is the bottle of lemon barley water which I saw his mum, a big fat, common looking lady, bring in yesterday. I unscrew the cap and pour it into the glass which stands on top of the locker, till the glass is half full. Then I fill it up to the top with water from the jug and start drinking as noisily as I can. It is so strong it makes my mouth want to cave in.

Suddenly there is a rustling down in the bed and Jerry's hair starts to appear from under the blankets, then his whole face, all covered in red crease marks from the sheet.

"You thieving shit face! Get off my drink!" he shouts, reaching for my hand which is holding the glass, but I dodge off the bed and behind the locker so he can't get me.

"I bet you'd like some," I say, taking another gulp, right in front of his nose.

He turns away, saying nothing, but I can tell he does want some really. I fill the glass back up to the top again with water from the jug and put it on the top of the locker.

Roger puts down his Eagle comic, which he has been watching us behind. "Can I have some?" he whines.

"No!" says Jerry, and gulps the whole glassful down in one go. He turns his back again. The door of his locker is still open and inside, it looks like our sideboard at home, because it seems to be absolutely crammed full of plates and saucers. I take out a big dinner plate from the bottom shelf and hold it up. In my locker I have one just like it, which I finished yesterday. The lady teacher gives you the little coloured mosaic pieces and you peel off the backing and stick them all in place. It took me two weeks to finish one plate, but Jerry looks as though he's got twenty in there.

"My God, Jerry, how long have you been in here?" I say.

He twists himself round on the bed and tries to snatch the stupid thing from me, but I keep a hold on it. He doesn't answer, he just gives me a long look as we both hold onto the plate, then he lets go. I put the plate back in the locker and close the door. Just as I am getting back into bed, Nurse de la Mare comes in. I think she saw me, but she doesn't say anything. She looks over at Jerry, who is lying back on his pillow with his eyes closed as though he has been like that all morning. She turns to me and looks serious, almost severe.

"How are your stitches today, Peter?" she says.

She pulls back the blankets to have a look. Her hands on my

tummy are as cool as the lino. Without looking at me, she says, "I think another day in bed would be advisable, Peter. Maybe you can get up tomorrow."

Suddenly I am screaming and shouting, "I want to get up! I want to get up! I want to get up!" over and over and I can't seem to stop. The room shrinks away from me and all I can hear is my own voice shouting, a long way off. Then, through my tears I can see very close to me, as though he has got out of bed and is sitting by my bedside, Jerry's pale face that is too big for his weak little body, and he looks very old. It's scary at first, because it seems like he is staring at me, but then I realise that he is looking right through me, taking a last look at the world, and he feels nothing for it and knows that he will not miss it. I wipe the tears from my eyes and listen to hear if I am still shouting, but the only sounds now are the swishing of the breeze and the creaking of the branches of The Cedar of Lebanon. Jerry and I are sitting somewhere near the top, swinging our legs out into the blue air. I turn to say something to him, but he gives his legs one big swing and lets go of the branch, his hair bursting out bright gold in the sun as he falls away from me.

***

A porter, or perhaps he is a male nurse, is rattling his trolley in through the porthole doors when I wake up. I shout to him to ask what day it is. I follow him with my eyes as he wheels it down the ward towards me.

"I should think you'd keep a low profile after last night's goings on," he says.

He leaves his trolley in the middle of the aisle where it will block the way completely and strolls over to my bed. "I hear you were a very naughty boy last night, Mr Grice. 'Bloody Foreign Whore', I'm told, you called Sister Mason. She's been called a few things in her time, but never Foreign. They had to send for Patrick and Livingstone to hold you down."

He looks at me, as though I am a bit of sputum in one of his kidney bowls. "Wouldn't have thought you had it in you," he says.

Behind me, the wood pigeon begins his crooning at the window which I cannot see. I ask the male nurse to turn my bed round, but he makes me swallow some kind of medicine that he has in a little cup, then he goes squeaking off, down towards the square windows.

***

That evening the wood pigeon came for the last time. I had split my stitches open again and could not have got up if I had wanted. He kept up his "cru, cru", all the time that Jerry was dying, then I heard the rustle of his wings and he was gone too. Through half closed eyes I could see Jerry's face, whiter than the pillow, and his crooked, breakable body still there under the blankets. They would think he was asleep. It occurred to me that Nurse de la Mare would be sad, and I wondered if she would cry. I thought crying might make her eyes even more beautiful.

When it is getting dark outside and the lights in the ward have been dimmed, with a great effort, I reach my right arm over to my bedside table and open the cupboard door. It is empty, except for a Gideon's Bible and two framed photographs of some children with gaps in their teeth. There are no plates; that's all over with now. I close the cupboard and switch on the anglepoise lamp which someone brought for me when I could still hold a book to ready by it. With some more effort I adjust the angle so that it shines brightly onto the shabby wall behind the beds on the opposite side of the ward. I bring both my hands up in front of my chest, so that the light catches them, making great, wobbly shadows on the wall. Carefully, and with some pain, I turn my hands so that they are back to back, and then I link my crooked thumbs together. There on the wall is my pigeon, fluttering his wings, his feathers like fingertips as he stretches them, preparing to fly.

## Robert Watson

### *Not My Little Girl*

She wasn't really late yet, though she could have been back fifteen minutes ago – just enough time to begin wavering in that nervous region between irritation and concern while he washed and cut vegetables. The potato skins softened and slipped off under his thumbs; grey, translucent pieces broke away easily to leave the smooth bodies more flesh-like, yellow and vulnerable as he set them on the draining board in a patch of sunlight. Carrot heads and gnarled orange fingers were swirling in the dirty water. It usually took her about twenty minutes to walk home from school, but it was a sunny afternoon and she sometimes dawdled, especially if she was with friends. There weren't any secluded lanes or sinister alleys, and there was just one busy road to cross.

Morales emptied the grimy water and scooped out the peelings and then glanced at the clock. She shouldn't waste time coming home while her mother was in hospital, but Morales reminded himself that he hadn't even put the dinner on yet. They wouldn't set off for a couple of hours. He dried his hands and studied a page in the cookery book again. He wanted to prove he could prepare a real dinner for two. He wanted to boast of it to his wife, and have his daughter confirm her father's little triumph, not because Frances thought him incapable but because she'd take pleasure in his transparent vanity. It would have been easier to use take-aways every night, but a take-away wouldn't remind her of their simple struggles at home. Morales didn't like it with his wife in hospital; it was a kind of dislocation, and it made him uneasy.

As soon as he heard the gate crunch back over the loose gravel drive Morales felt the release of several unclarified tensions – his daughter was home, they wouldn't be late at the hospital, the meal would surely cook itself well now. He looked out of the kitchen window and after a few seconds saw the top of Maria's head going by, rather slowly.

The back door opened, then the inner door. Maria came into the kitchen dragging her satchel on the quarry tiles.

"What's wrong?" Morales asked with a smile.

"Nothing."

"Something is," he insisted gently, not approaching her yet, though she liked to be hugged or kissed usually, and since her mother's absorbing pregnancy she had grown even more sensitive, sometimes babyish and clinging. But this afternoon she hadn't met her father's gaze and seemed to be swaying slightly, as if deciding whether to submit to a sympathetic interrogation or make a break for the stairs.

"I'm about to put the dinner on," Morales said. "I've kept the peelings if you want to see how the rabbits like them. Maybe you should wash first. What do you think? Then we'll visit your mother and your new baby brother right after we've eaten. How's that?"

He was talking too much, deliberately, because he believed that if anyone in the family had a bad day the best way of getting over it was to enfold them in the affairs of home as soon as possible. Morales hadn't settled into marriage until his mid-thirties, and he'd known loneliness and how isolating it felt not to have any loving support. His children would never have to flounder with no one to turn to, he was sure of that. The family was the most important thing. But Maria hadn't come out of her gloom.

"It's not fair," she said petulantly, letting go her bag and at last looking at her father so he could see she'd been crying all the way home. She was not crying any more, though. She was furious.

Morales held a clean cloth under the cold tap.

"Here," he offered, "let me wipe your face."

His daughter approached him cautiously, not wanting to sniffle again. He knelt, taking one of her small hot hands in his and dabbing the damp cloth over the dirty tear-smears on her cheeks. He could feel Maria's clenched outrage, and immediately his mind boiled with recalled injustices he'd either suffered or observed down the years. Morales knew the symptoms and was ready to launch an attack at any offender, ready to enfold Maria and defend her and wipe out the world for her.

At the same time, curiously, he realised that he was reluctant to hear anything, almost resentful. The sunny day had darkened in his head. There was the meal and then there was the visit, he didn't want anything more complicated; he didn't want anything nasty at all. Morales already knew more than he needed about the futility of seeking to repossess justice. It seemed to him he'd had a lifetime of being let down and being unable to set things straight. It wasn't because he was feeble, it was the way things went. But for a long time now, since his marriage, in fact, everything had been positive. So he'd forgotten to keep his guard up. Obviously something had been bound to go wrong soon. At least the baby had been born okay, though, and his wife was fine. But Morales should have known his elation couldn't last.

Within seconds he had given himself an emotional roller-coaster of frustrating confrontations with deaf authority figures, he had argued soundlessly on doorsteps with the loutish parents of thuggish sons, he had dealt with bullying, extortion, drugs and, God forbid, sexual advances. He had no idea what was bothering Maria, and his determination to sort it out and make her happy again didn't leave him, but by the time he'd cleaned her face he felt exhausted.

"I didn't do anything, Dad," Maria complained. "It's not fair. Me and Karen and Helena were all told off by Mr Potts, and we *told* him it wasn't us, but he wouldn't believe us. He said we were liars. He said we'd been identified."

"That sounds horrible," Morales said, still sympathetically, though he began to be wary. "What is it you're supposed to have done?"

"We *didn't*, Dad, honestly! We *wouldn't*!"

"All right," he soothed, for the time being. "All right."

She was desperate to be innocent, and not only innocent but actually incapable of whatever it was, and that made Morales almost seasick. Even the most angelic children were not angels, and all children were capable of doing childlike things, naturally. Guilt could express itself in protestations of that kind, he knew that from experience and prepared himself for the possibility that Maria had been caught out doing something they'd both be ashamed of, something he'd have to promise not to tell her mother, at least not just yet. What could it be? Not bullying, certainly. Maria didn't have enough insensitivity. She couldn't be vicious. Not a sexual misadventure either, not yet. What, then? Something minor but definitely wrong. Pilfering? It was impossible. Morales had stolen from a shop once, and been caught. He still burned whenever he remembered.

What would the next move be? For her own sake he would let her know at once that it wasn't the end of the world, and that the best thing to do was face up to it and apologise where necessary, and then make a clean start. Obviously Maria was deeply shocked because Mr Potts hadn't believed her or her friends, and probably that was the worst of it, realising that the adults you had to trust no longer trusted you. Again, she'd feel disorientated by that if she was innocent or guilty. Maybe her capacity to be hurt in such a way constituted punishment enough, but Morales wasn't going to make light of it. Maria had to understand that Potts was right, but she could still be reassured. He could let her know he didn't like Potts any more than anyone else did. Potts was a jerk. If Maria had done wrong it was a serious matter, only her father didn't intend to be too severe. He hoped everything could be resolved by the time they reached the hospital.

"It was after school yesterday," Maria started. "This woman said she was driving past outside school and saw the three of us making rude signs at her and laughing and calling out bad words. It *wasn't* us, Dad!"

"Who's the woman? Does she know you? Do we know her?"

"We haven't been able to see her. Mr Potts said she came in this morning and identified us coming from assembly, but she can't have, because we didn't do it."

"I don't get this," Morales admitted, already relieved it was nothing more serious and agitated because it was nothing he had a chance of resolving. "Tell me, what are you most upset about?"

"Everything. It's horrible that Mr Potts thinks we lied and won't listen when we tell the truth. It's horrible being accused of making dirty signs, because I know that's wrong and I don't do it. It's not fair, Dad. It's not right. I don't want to go back tomorrow."

Morales wondered what he could do. Throwing a hand signal at a passing motorist was hardly a major crime and Maria must have seen him do it occasionally. On the other hand it was uncouth, and his daughter was idealistic enough to be as self-righteously innocent as she claimed.

"Listen," he said reasonably, "I'll phone Mr Potts and have a word with him, if you like, but first I want to be absolutely sure about this. I know you're honest, and it's not like you to do anything like that, but if you were with your friends and did it anyway I wouldn't be mad at you. Do you understand? I'd be much happier if you admitted it and decided never to do it again. If I phone him I want to be absolutely certain you're not just too ashamed to own up."

"I didn't do anything wrong, Dad," Maria said in the awful, flat, low, depressed tone of someone who had lost hope of ever being believed again. She looked soulfully at her father, as if he was the one who had finally betrayed her. She had gone beyond feeling sorry for herself and now seemed to be pitying him for his sad lack of faith.

"Fair enough, then," he tried to say jauntily, but it was obvious he'd made matters worse by attempting a balanced understanding of the affair.

Morales stood and rubbed his knees. He threw the cloth into the sink. His daughter left her school bag on the floor and shut herself in the toilet. He thought she'd probably stay there until dinner was ready, or at least until he'd phoned Mr Potts. There was really no way of avoiding that, though Morales knew in advance what he was going to sound like. His wife was a teacher, and she'd told him how foolish some parents could be at parents' evenings, when it was necessary to draw attention to their children's occasional short-comings. Most were sensible, but a few would be adamantly defensive, incapable of believing their sons or daughters could transgress in any way whatever. He was going to sound like one of those parents, and Potts would handle him tactfully, with professional condescension, and nothing would be achieved. Certain kinds of communication were simply impossible. Morales took a deep breath and pulled a chair close to the phone.

"My daughter's just come home in a terrible state," he explained, as if he were talking to another sympathetic parent. "I've spoken to her, and listened to what she has to say, and I'm as sure as I can be that Maria has been mistaken for somebody else." That didn't sound over-protective, he thought; it was one adult to another, impartial and fair.

"You don't sound convinced, Mr Morales," Potts chuckled urbanely.

Morales could never have got a tone like that into his voice. It had nothing to do with the larynx, but started way back in the satin-draped chambers of the ego. Potts just couldn't help sounding better-informed than everyone else. He didn't know what uncertainty was. No one had ever told him it was normal. That was why men like him were secure in authority. The knowing, disparaging chuckle was part of the radical ignorance of nuance that equipped him for keeping parents and children in their place. As soon as Morales heard it he felt at once angry and impotent.

"It's just that I know children aren't always as blameless as parents want to think. My wife's a teacher, too." He was struggling. He felt his mouth was far too close to Potts's ear. He could almost smell the man's after shave, see the shine of his chin, hear the suave breathing. "I'm trying to be objective."

"But this is a serious matter," Potts surprised him by saying. It was effortless, if you didn't listen to people. "You may not agree, but I take a very dim view of children who gesture at passing cars."

"Well I do, too, of course," Morales was compelled to follow on defensively. He was hot all over, protesting yet obviously guilty, unable to control the situation. He remembered his key point: "But I don't think she did it."

"I'm afraid she did." There was no opening. "For obvious reasons I don't intend to name the woman who complained, but she was in no doubt – she saw the three girls, Mr Morales, and your daughter was one of them."

"Yet Maria says she hasn't seen this woman yet. I don't understand how they could have been picked out without any of them even seeing her. I'm very unhappy about this. My daughter insists she's innocent, and has no reason to lie. I believe her. She's distraught because you don't. If you're wrong, think of the consequence for a child's confidence."

"Children are surprisingly resilient, Mr Morales," Potts said in the same nimbly offhand way, as if anything Morales told him had to be discounted at once. Then his tone changed slightly. Perhaps his tea was getting cold. "Are you suggesting that a woman would come to complain out of sheer malice, and then choose three girls at random? Or is your reasoning that she must be a liar because children never lie?"

Morales was stumped. He fought hard against losing his temper; he was determined not to concede that Maria had been wrong, and in the confusion he heard himself explaining how he'd been preparing vegetables for dinner because his wife had just had a baby. Before he could stop himself he changed course and told Potts he was pompous and unfit to take responsibility for the welfare of children. Even rabbits, he added crazily, were too impressionable to be risked under Potts's tutelage. It was exhilarating but counter-productive. The next thing Morales heard was the long silky satisfied sigh of a man who now knew precisely where the appalling little girl had come by her manners. Potts was far too smooth to say it, though.

"I don't think that's helpful, do you?" he asked in quiet triumph. "I'm afraid our children aren't always as blameless as we'd like to believe." He paused to let the message sink in. "I'm sure she won't do it again."

"Look, I *know* all that!" Morales cried. "That's what I said to *you*! But Maria didn't... Oh, what's the use!"

He hung up abruptly, in a murderous rage, and smiled wanly at his daughter as she emerged from the toilet at the end of the hall. She seemed to comprehend everything, and now that her father was suffering she brightened up a bit.

Dinner was not a great success. The meat pies were fine at the edges, frozen at the heart. The potatoes seemed to be raw and lukewarm. The sprouts and carrots were succulent, but neither of them cared for sprouts and carrots. For pudding they had cheesecake, which Morales had bought, and that was fine. They wrapped half to take to the hospital.

By the time they arrived the car parks were full and Morales had to take a chance pulling on to the pavement. He made sure there would be plenty of room for ambulances to get by, and the pavement was still wide enough for a wheelchair to squeeze past. Morales was a thoughtful man. Maria carried the cheesecake. She was a good girl, behaving as though nothing had spoilt her day. She kissed her mother and held her hand and said she was looking after her father as well as she could. Morales grinned and nodded. While Maria made soppy noises at her baby brother he asked his wife how her day had been and listened sympathetically to the tales of indignity, farce and tragedy which made up life in a maternity ward.

"Is everything all right?" Frances asked. "You've got that frown."

"Oh, sure," he replied airily, and smiled sunnily. "I need more practice with the cooker, though."

"We need a new cooker. It doesn't heat through evenly."

"Yeah." He diverted his irritation to the institution. "Why can't we pick him up, though?"

He knew the answer: petty authority. Relatives from outside were liable to bring germs in. The newborn had to be protected. On the first day he had been allowed to hold his baby, under a nurse's watchful gaze, as long as he was wearing a gown and a mask over his mouth and nose. Morales looked down the long ward, then asserted himself. He reached into the see-through cot and picked up his son and cradled him defiantly, and spoke to him gently, and tried to get him to grip his finger.

"He's looking at me," Morales said ecstatically.

No one told him off. Frances beamed at them both, and Maria came close as well. They were united in their quiet, private joy.

"One more day," Frances said when he told her how much he was missing her. There was a bell that rang to make the fathers leave. Morales and Maria lingered, but they couldn't ignore it.

The car had been wheel-clamped.

"Bastards!" Morales muttered. "It couldn't have been in anyone's bloody way – what were we supposed to do? Abandon the visit?"

"Never mind, Dad."

Maria was supportive, but it was an unnecessary fine, and an unnecessary inconvenience. An hour or so later, when Maria was ready for bed, Morales raised the subject of Potts again, tactfully, because his daughter had obviously calmed down now, and might be ready to confess, assuming she'd lied before.

She was reluctant, but once started just as convincing, just as upset about being disbelieved. Morales apologised sincerely, and admitted that he couldn't do anything to make the head teacher more understanding. He believed his daughter was too young to have to learn such a dispiriting lesson in mediocrity and frustration, and he wanted to cry for her.

They made up names for her brother for a while.

The sad thing about it all, Morales realised, was that he would never know for certain whether or not Maria had been truthful. Whether or not she'd *done* it mattered less. Either way a small bond of absolute trust had been broken, and it could never be made good. Even if the mysterious woman who'd complained changed her mind about who was responsible Morales would still know it had been possible to lack faith in his daughter's word. And that man Potts, similarly, would always retain his prejudice about Maria's father – a hothead, an over-protective, abusive problem-parent – and therefore about Maria herself. Justice can't be repossessed. Potts must have entered something on a report already, a note, dated, permanent. Nothing like that was ever erased.

"Maria," Morales said softly before leaving her to sleep, "when I lost my temper with Mr Potts, and at the hospital, that was wrong of me, you know. But – well, I have to say it made me feel pretty good for a moment!"

His daughter's eyes were closed, but she started a smile. Morales did, too. He kissed her nose and said goodnight, and realised he'd overcome his black mood. As long as it's us against them, he grinned to himself.

In the kitchen he washed up, then carefully wrote down the names Maria had suggested for her brother. He was glad he'd defied the hospital's hygienic regulations and dared to pick up his own son.

Morales wasn't a rebellious man, and in some ways he accepted he was ineffectual, but he did at least have a good family, and they gave him strength. Even if Potts didn't believe him, even if the car was clamped, his son had looked into his eyes and made him a giant.

"Did I wake you, Mr Potts?" he asked innocently. "Good," he added. "Listen. You were wrong about my daughter. She's a Morales. Now go back to sleep."

He disconnected the phone and sat for a long time in the darkness, glad he hadn't crumbled, not ashamed to have done something a bit stupid, almost happy, just wishing Frances and his son were home to complete everything. He giggled. It wasn't the sanctimonious sound Potts would have made, and perhaps it was a touch vindictive, but Morales realised he didn't care, because he was a family man and he hadn't been crushed. He raised his hand and made a gesture at the phone, and grinned in the dark.

## Philip Young

*Dragonfly*

Her room was just paintings. I counted them, I don't know why. Numbers don't matter much, do they?

"Bank account numbers matter. Telephone numbers matter."

"Well, yes, but they're just numbers."

"Mm, hh."

There were nineteen – six on the wall by the door; just three by the window; seven on the wall in front of me, all different sizes. And there were three behind me.

"They're beautiful. You're good, really good. I like them."

"I think I'm going to stop soon. I think I have painted enough."

"What do you mean?"

"You ask a lot of questions."

"I ask too many."

"Really?"

"Mm, hh."

"Let's play Twenty Questions. It's my favourite game. I think you can learn everything you ever need to know about somebody if you ask them the right twenty questions."

"OK, let's do it. You go first."

"Would you like a drink?"

"Is that an official question?"

She smiled: "Probably not."

"Well, in that case, yeah, I would. Please. Thanks."

"I've got some wine. Only red."

"I only drink red."

"You see! I only asked one question and I learnt two things. It's easy."

"Ah, but that's not official knowledge. It doesn't count."

She started to pour. The nicest Spanish wine I have tasted. "Who goes first?"

"It's your game Danette, I think it is only fair if you start. Fire away."

"OK. Alright." She looked at me with those put your hand in the fire and you won't feel a thing eyes. "I forget to tell you, there's a rule that you have to tell the truth – death or glory. My first question is – does that bother you?"

"If we are telling the truth – yes, it does. It's got to." I laughed, and I took a drink.

"Your turn..."

I pointed to the painting by the door. "Who's that?"

"Aagh, it's awful, isn't it? My very first one. A Portrait of Virginity. I try to forget it."

"What do you mean?"

She shook her head. "Sorry, no supplementaries – that one doesn't count. It's my turn again."

I emptied my glass, and poured another.

"I can't help it. I'm just curious. I want to know all about you."

If you'd seen Danette you would understand what I meant, the way I felt. It was snowing in July, and I was drinking wine with just an angel and there was no way I was going to be getting back on the train. Really I ought to have telephoned, but I didn't seem to have the time.

She was saying: "I've told you, you can find out all you want with twenty questions. It just takes a little imagination."

"OK, go on then. It's you again."

"What's the best pair of shoes you have ever worn?"

I stretched out my feet. "These." Beautiful soft red leather, soft as slippers, with pointed toes and side-laces. The sole was coming loose and they'd been in the cupboard because I couldn't bring myself to throw them away. They were so good I even felt like nailing them to the wall like a picture but I'd never got round to it. I couldn't believe I'd pulled them out for the first time in ages and this was their last trip.

"O-oh really. I'm glad you did. I saw you walking down the corridor in them, all toes. That's why I came to talk to you. It's always the first thing I notice."

I kept drinking the wine because it was so nice but I really didn't want to get drunk because I wanted to remember all this.

"If he was the first, which was the second?"

"Gianni. He's just up here. He's walking away with my white glove in his back pocket because that's the way he was, nothing ever really lasted."

I had never seen a girl with eyes like hers. When she looked at me I would have answered anything, told her secrets I would never have told anybody.

"Which do you prefer – black on white or white on black?"

I thought, so what; so this: "White on white. Just a little bit more than black on black. Which one is number three?"

"Just there, behind you. One of my favourites. John. He was a painter, he taught me a lot."

John was smiling and I didn't like that.

"Do you describe your glass as half-full or half-empty?"

"I dunno. I just like to think there's a back-up on the bar waiting either way." She poured me another and I asked about her fourth.

She pointed. "Jack. I met him hitch-hiking. Mm, hh."

It was all messy and out of control, but I liked it one of the best.

"If you were a squirrel, would you be grey and eat acorns and be successful, or would you be red and threatened?"

"No contest. Undoubtedly red, glamorous and lazy." I wanted to know so much about her – I wanted facts: how old she was, how tall she was, how soft she was. I wanted magic: how does she feel, where was she going, would she buy me the birthday present I always wanted?

But it felt so much safer to stick to my formula. That way I gave nothing away. "Who is number five?"

"Ah, that's Tom. I met him flicking coins on a street corner. Everyone loves a loser."

I don't want you to love me because I'm a loser. I'm not a loser. I am a winner.

And she asked: "Why are dragonflies so important to you?"

"I like dragonflies because their beauty is so fragile, so fleeting, but it is so undeniable. The real problem with beauty is that it's not constant, it changes."

"Mm, hh. But your questions don't change much, do they? I am not sure you are playing the game."

I shrugged my shoulders, and curled my lip in that special way. "There's no rule against it, is there?"

"Suppose not. So I have to answer you truthfully. Number six is over there. It's Albert. He was a photographer, he worked for this weird magazine."

He was so flabby and naked. "I can't imagine anybody standing and being painted like that."

"It's easy, try it some time." She laughed, then she bit her thumb, and got terribly serious. "What does an etymologist like you feel like when you accidentally crush a beetle?"

"Well, the etymologist in me doesn't really care, but the entomologist can get quite upset. Insects mean more to me than words."

"Ah, very clever."

I hoped I hadn't offended her but I hate it when people use the wrong word. "Tell me about the seventh."

"That's Eugene, on the wall behind you. He was a writer, but he got too caught up in things. Sometimes it's better to know you've got a return ticket in your back pocket."

I didn't want to know about Eugene.

"If you could own a painting, would it be an Elstir or Degas?"

"Elstir – I am always happier with fiction than reality." And I know who my favourite painter is now. I know what I want to hang on my wall.

But my game was beginning to worry me; maybe I was learning too much. I thought maybe I should ask her what her favourite colour was, get it over with. I poured her another glass of wine, and contemplated moving a little closer.

But it would have been wrong, not playing the game. "After Eugene..."

Her expression changed. I had asked a hard question.

"Oh, he was Norman, the corrupter of my youth. I still know him; maybe you have read...?" But she seemed to change her mind and she said: "Do you read?"

Of course I had the Bestiary of Dragonflies in my pocket, but I thought I would save that for later. This could have been a chance to impress, to reel off so many names, but this was Danette, and she'd have known all along.

"There's a man I know who goes into my favourite pub and at lunchtime there's usually just me and him and we are both reading books so we always say hello. He is always reading these great big thick science-fiction things that are tetrologies or something. Sometimes he comes in and I'm not reading, and he says 'Are you still reading?' and I think what a stupid question – if I had stopped reading how would I know which end of the cornflake packet to open?"

I thought maybe this would make her laugh. I realised that although her face was so alive she hadn't laughed much so I supposed it must have been my fault because clearly she could laugh a lot.

But she kept talking. And I kept listening, if only because that was a good reason to look at her.

I suppose I haven't told you what Danette looked like. Normally I find it really hard to remember faces but I remember hers so well...

"Norman paid for me to go to Barcelona. Wanted me to learn about Gaudi and architecture and hidden beauty but I learnt to paint portraits on fingernails.

"I was glad to get away." And just for a moment she hesitated, like she had just remembered she had forgotten something important and it was too late to go back.

"So, which one was ...?"

"Number nine? By the window. Julio. I just saw him in this bar, El Mercadillo. He was wearing a black leather jacket, with one arm painted, delicately, with white seagulls on azure blue so small that at first it looked like faded denim. His t-shirt was squares of wood, painted magenta, held together with gold chain. I was feeling brave, and I said 'I have got to paint you'. I spent hours, drinking carajillo, painting. But in the night he chewed his fingernails and it was all ruined."

I didn't want to hear this. "I think it's your question – come on."

"Alright." I don't think she wanted to be interrupted.

"If you wrote a book tonight, what would it be about?"

"It would be about an insect that started life as a larvae, a grub – what a word – grub – that nobody found beautiful, not even me, but one day it hatched, after months and months, into a glistening flying diamond, with just five minutes to make love and die..."

And it took me a moment to gather my stride – you see, I'm not ugly. I said: "Ten?"

And I had this awful fear that I hadn't said 'please'. Ten please Danette; me please Danette.

"C'est Marcel Dubedout. He was a clown, working outside Beaubourg. We used to spend the day together going up and down that escalator on the side of the Pompidou Centre. He used to talk too loud about the symbolism of people inside tubes and I used to get in everybody's way trying to sketch him, and by the time we reached the top I'd always be able to sell it to somebody. Worked every time."

She leaned over, poured me some wine. Why was she telling me this story?

"What's your favourite word?"

"Erotic." And as soon as I had said it I felt flushed with guilt. It sounded so obvious, so trite. "That was your eleventh question; you know more than half of everything there is to know about me."

"Mm, hh. I told you it was a good game."

I wanted to talk to her about something else, but I just said: "Et numéro onze?"

"C'est n'est-pas onze. He was English. Terribly English. He was A Disaster. I think my embarrassment shows, don't you? He was called Chris. I met him in a nightclub. I only wanted do him because he was so artificial."

And everything about him was like those actors who are so ugly and you wonder how they managed before they found that one part that could make their ugliness glamorous.

"Which word do you hate most?"

"I hate all words that are slimy, but I hate 'such' most."

"That's bizarre!"

"But true."

"Such is life." She giggled.

I think that was her first joke, but somehow she made me laugh all the time. I felt like telling her. I giggled, and said: "I think we are up to twelve."

Danette clapped her hands together, then flopped back in to her chair. "Ken. Just because he was so... so hirsute, and that made it so difficult for me. A challenge, I suppose you could say." She rolled her eyes, like she was giving nothing away. "It's my question, and I am going to be a thief – who do you think was Thirteen?"

"I think he is there above the fireplace." I had been looking at him all night. The fragile green dragonfly.

"Mm, hh. The Green Dandy. Do you really?"

Every question I asked her, her mood changed. I should have found it disconcerting, but I didn't. It just made her more attractive.

"I really do, but – you tell me – who was lucky thirteen?"

"You were right. That was some weird sin. He was special. Still is. You are getting to know me, too."

"Mm, hh..."

"My question: How could you tell it was him?"

"It was obvious; you are a good painter." I wanted to know his name, and she hadn't told me.

I felt angry: "How about fourteen..."

"Aahmhm. This one's a bit embarrassing. Beppo. That's what he called himself. I let him spoil something rather special."

I hated the look of regret in her eyes. The special thing, it was Thirteen, wasn't it? I wanted to, but I didn't ask. There were seven to go and I didn't want to know.

See, Danette was right; she was learning about the real me. But what was I learning? I hadn't got the nerve to ask her any of the real questions. She was learning more about me because my questions were all a big cop out than she was from anything I said.

It was snowing in July. A couple of hours before I was sitting on a train listening to power station spotters – I was going to write that down in my notebook, for another day, because I had never heard something so stupid before as power station spotting, and now I'm here with this angel and all I can think of to say is that when I was little I had a rabbit called George after George Best and it was something I always wanted to write a book about, or at least a story, and that I remember watching Watch With Mother and the Flowerpot Men were given three wishes and I knew that my third wish would have been for a magic something or other like a brooch or even just a stone that I could rub and any wish I made would be granted. Sounded a great idea to me at the time, so clever for a little boy.

Still does. She clicked her fingers: "If you were a Flowerpot Man, would you be Bill, or would you be Ben?"

"Ben." I said it quite confidently, it just came to me, but who could have a favourite Flowerpot Man? What did it matter? What had I given away? I felt so exposed. There was only one thing to say: "Quindici?"

"Funfzehn! It was all so terribly messy, the Beppo business. Norman gave me another ticket and I went to Berlin. Met a bloke in a shopping centre with a lion cub on a chain. I did it just to prove my nerve hadn't gone."

I was puzzled. "But where's the lion?"

She looked hurt. "It's not there, but if you can't see it, the painting's failed."

She didn't even look at me when she asked: "If you were Ben and you had those three wishes, and you were down to your last wish, what would you wish for?"

"That's hard because I have two wishes at the moment. But I suppose I'd wish for a magic glass of wine that was always full and always granted me my wishes."

She poured.

"We are up to, errm, sechzehn?"

"Actually it's seize. He's the top right, Jazzbeau. He played such sad saxophone in a bar in Lyon. I just sat there with my sketchbook in the corner."

And she got up, and turned on the tape recorder. It sounded all deep like Lester Young, but I knew who it was and I wished it would end.

"This isn't very modest, but which of them do you like best?"

How could I answer that? "They say practice makes perfect, so perhaps I'll like your next one most."

I can't play poker, but I think I just upped the stakes.

"How about seventeen?"

"Mm, hh. Philip. He was just a journalist. Didn't fool me for a moment." And she laughed, first time for a while (I had been counting).

"If someone painted you, which would be the most important – that it looked like you or he chose the right colour?"

'He' choose? I don't want 'him' to paint me. I want you. You know I want you.

"The colour." She knew I was lying. Just a bit, but lying and that broke the rules. I nearly admitted it, but I said: "Eighteen?" There were only two pictures left.

"Eric. He was just a rock and roller in an Iggy Pop I Wanna Be Your Dog t-shirt and buckled black boots. I was trying to recapture my youth, but all the music made my ears hurt and I knew his kitchen would be a pit."

"So's mine. Your question?"

"If someone said you were quite handsome, would you notice the 'quite' or the 'handsome'?"

Was this a compliment? "I would notice the someone."

Danette smiled. I smiled: "It's my nineteenth question, and there's only the one over there."

It's a smart young businessman in a black pinstripe Hugo Boss suit, a striped, button-down shirt, hand painted silk tie, hand-me-down shoes and a slouch hat that covered his face. She was unmistakable, but I asked: "Who is it?"

And she said: "Don't you know?"

I shrugged on my shoulders and curled my lip. She pulled on a hat and covered her face. "My bid for realism."

But even Danette couldn't capture the beauty of her own eyes, so I said: "I hate realism."

"So, my twentieth question; can you guess?"

"Mm, hh..." And I was so happy.

"Can I paint you?"

"As long as you get my colour right."

"Hey-la-la."

"Now?"

"Yeah, why not?"

She said sit by the window and read a book. So I pulled the Bestiary and opened it at random, and started reading.

"For the male dragonfly, sex is a matter of both taking and giving. The unique structure of the dragonfly penis allows the male to remove another male's sperm from the female's reproductive tract before he inserts his own."

Danette was cleaning her brushes and straightening the canvas; I was trying to look serious and sexy. "So it is that an insect which typically spends twenty minutes in the act of copulation, devotes the first nineteen to clearing out sperm from the female's previous matings."

## Moe Sherrard-Smith

### *Geese Flight*

Twice the dream of wild geese had disturbed Ranja's sleep. She knew if it came a third time her spirit must prepare to fly away with them.

She had heard her grandfather Harunka speak of the thrice dream. Harunka, the wise one, steeped in the ways and lores of Eskimo tradition, had given her the knowledge. All the stored knowledge of her life had come from that old man. He taught her to bear grief and accept the Eskimo's birthright by living from season to season. Even the twentieth century couldn't change that fact.

Grief had been no stranger to Ranja's young seasons. She remembered the coming of Spring, her fourth or fifth Spring, and the softly moaning procession of fur-clad men bearing home two bodies. One, the huge white polar bear, a cause for rejoicing. There would be food, oil, and a warm fur. The other, a bundle of grief. Ranja's father, a victim of the beast. The endless harsh cycle of Eskimo life alternated grief and rejoicing.

Always it seemed to Ranja that Spring made the cycle harsher. Spring heralded changes, not always welcome.

Two Springs passed after her father's death, then grandfather Harunka took her to one side and made her a bed in his hut.

Ranja, puzzled, watched her mother's hut. Why had her mother sent her away? Mother, strong and wise like Harunka, had taught Ranja many things. The ways of the woman, and the ways of the man – the son there had never been born to her and her beloved husband.

It was then that Harunka had explained. "When the wild geese come thrice in the dream, it is time for an Eskimo's Spirit to fly with them. We must not become a burden to the community. We cannot feed extra mouths, and those too old or too ill to work are called to fly."

Ranja knew her mother was not old, not as old as Harunka and many of the other women, but about her mother hung an air of endings. An incurable sadness, a resignation. This must be the sickness of which her grandfather spoke.

Her mother came to the child and held her tightly, wrapping her in the polar bear skin. From her mother's eyes flowed salt tears. Ranja took them on her tongue and into herself for remembrance. With no word, her mother returned to her own hut.

That afternoon the dogs began to whine and circle, sniffing the air. The sky gave no clue, but the dogs heard the whisper on the wind. The storm was coming.

It came. For three days it raged. When it abated, Ranja's mother had gone. "Flown with the geese," said grandfather. Only later did Ranja come to understand that her mother had chosen deliberately to walk out into the storm and die. For the second time in her life, Ranja cried.

Weeping now for her mother, as she had for her father. Harunka took her tears to comfort her grief.

Ranja grew through many Springs and came into womanhood. Before he had his thrice dream, Harunka found her a good husband. Laneyka, a fine, handsome youth, strong, fierce. They had five children, one each Spring of their early married life. One son died before the next one came. Two boys and two girls they raised to a healthy childhood. Three more babies died in Ranja's womb. The family was complete, Harunka knew. "It is the Great Spirit's way of saying enough."

Laneyka, her husband, often laughed at Ranja's folklore. And as the Springs passed, she saw him grow less inclined to the hardships of Eskimo life.

Life was changing.

The coming of the White Man was a seductive sickness. He brought his electricity, frozen foods, cooking stoves, television, oil pipelines and easy jobs in his settlements.

"Once an Eskimo, always an Eskimo," she told Laneyka, "you are born to the ways of our people."

"The ways are hard for my bones," he grumbled. "In two, maybe three Winters, the White Man will pay me enough money to buy us a house in their city. We shall be warm, we shall eat well and we shall not have to endure the cold Winters here."

Ranja shook her head. No, she could not go to the White Man's city. She did not want his sickness of endless noise, perpetual light. Heritage had taught her the wisdom of Winter. Dark and renewal. Silence: for man and land. Harunka had rarely spoken then. A gesture, or a hand laid on her shoulder sufficed. And in the long dark, the Spirit, or whatever innermost being he acknowledged, roamed free in his mind to adventure the ways of rebirth. So it was for her.

No, she had seen too many young men of her tribe succumb to

the sickness. They returned sometimes to visit but although their bodies lived, in their eyes was only death. Death of Spirit. Through the quick babble of words tumbling from their lips, Ranja observed they had nothing to say. White Man's fire water had blurred reactions when there was no need to hunt caribou or fish through ice.

So Laneyka left, taking with him the younger son and daughter, Haunja and Janu.

That Winter, Ranja's Spirit grew more and more restless. It wandered far, she was sure it was in search of Harunka. The wise old man had taught her many things but all his experience had not prepared her for this new kind of grief that the split in her family caused.

Laneyka came home many times at first. Then his visits grew less. Ranja saw in his face the same dead eyes.

"I'm saving for a house, a fine house." His voice carried a false enthusiasm. Ranja received money from him, though she needed little. But where was the rest? Had he not promised her a fine house in two or three Winters? The time had nearly come, but his heart was in the oil city.

"And my son and daughter?" she asked of him.

He brought her photographs. Haunja, a tall, dark boy, nay a man, in blue jeans, bright woollen jacket. Only his colour betrayed the roots of this otherwise White Man. Ranja sewed his likeness into the skin of the polar bear. Let her son belong with her dead father, he was lost to her.

Janu's likeness she couldn't bear to keep. A painted face, smiling mouth, breasts almost bared and many men around her. How could Ranja keep a likeness such as this? This woman was no issue of Harunka's tribe. She was a devil her people called an Eskimo whore. A whore with the same dead eyes of her son and husband. "How is your daughter become this?" she demanded.

Laneyka had no answer. "Drugs and prostitution I do not understand myself. She will not listen to me."

"Come back to your people, Laneyka. Bring home the children. Come back and listen to the wind, walk the land. Time will heal your sickness."

"Soon." There was no conviction. "You must visit the city. Use the aeroplane, it is quicker than four days by dog sled. I will show you my place in the camp, they call it a dormitory. I will take you to the bars. We can drink with my friends."

She placed a hand on his shoulder but said nothing.

When Laneyka returned to his camp, she harnessed the dog sled. There was no desire in her to get into the White Man's aeroplane and go to his city. What she needed was the wind shrieking to her its supremacy, reminding her of her heritage, her dependence.

Soon her eldest son, Laneylika, took himself a wife. A Christian, half white girl, Mary. Ranja took them into her home. What use to build another when this housed only one old woman?

For the wedding, Laneyka paid his last visit home. Ranja didn't say goodbye when he left. She took his bloated face in her hands and leaned to his thickened, flabby body. The tears flowed copiously for Laneyka, the young, muscular husband, the man of her dreams, the father of her children. She washed his face with her tears to safeguard his Spirit. His clothes were ragged and he spoke no more of his job. Nor did the money come. It was her son Haunja who sent the money, who told her that Laneyka lived in the streets, begging drinks, refusing his son's help. He would not, could not, return.

Nor was her son to return. He had worked, improved himself. "I am a foreman now, old mother. I ask you, as my father asked you, come to my house in the city. There is nothing I can do for him, but I can take care of you."

"No my son. It pleases my heart that you are happy but my ways are those of my people. That is why I cannot help Laneyka: he does not believe."

In due time Laneylika and Mary produced a child. Presents from the tribe showered on the couple.

"We are so few now that any child is a cause for rejoicing," Ranja told them. She took the child in her hands. "You are an Eskimo. Be faithful to your people." And softly, beneath her breath she whispered, "stay with us, little one." Her thoughts fluttered briefly to the city and the child she had never seen. The daughter of her daughter. A fatherless child that Janu was ashamed to bring to the tribe. Half white, disowned by both races, condemned to be an alien whichever way she turned.

Laneylika and Mary smiled back at Ranja. This son was Ranja's pride. A hunter, a fisher, a skin trader and also a shopkeeper – Mary's idea. He and his wife worked long and hard. Unlike his brother and sister, he showed no willingness to forsake his people and live in the city. He was the child ever-willing to listen to his mother's folklore.

Lately though, the arguments grew harder.

"We have to adapt something of the White Man's ways, old mother. There is not enough wild food for us. We are forbidden to hunt the white bear, the caribou has left because it too cannot find food. We need medicines for our sicknesses, for our children. When little Ranja returns she will be a fine doctor."

"Your sister may not return." The day the missionaries had persuaded Ranja to let them finance her eldest daughter through medical school, Ranja heard the dogs howl. Howl at the loss. She, and they, they knew little Ranja would find no happiness in returning.

"You must let the doctor see you," Laneylika insisted, "he will know what your pains are, and he will put the sight back in your eyes. You can barely see in the Winter."

"Winter is not for seeing, my son. Winter will cure what ails me. And if not, I must do as my mother did. Harunka the wise knew all these things."

"Old mother, I forbid you to walk out into the snow to die. It's old-fashioned, it's barbaric. You must get strong. We need you to care for the child. Mary has little strength. She has the milk fever, that is why the doctor is coming soon."

"The ways of our people will cure Mary. Shadows and silence, the oil of seal and fish."

Ranja was not to win. She tried to resist their pressure but Mary's half white nature tugged too strongly at Laneylika's reason. The white doctor put into Mary a needle filled with milky white fluid. He gave her tablets. Then he made arrangements to take her and the baby away to the city for three weeks.

"Read this card, please," he commanded Ranja before he left.

Ranja shook her head. "I do not read." Were these city men so lacking in knowledge of her people? She had confused him. "I will tell you what I see through the window." Did he understand her words? The joy of seeing snow melting, crying silently back into the land. She could tell of the children on their snow mobiles. How those machines barked. Better for an Eskimo that dogs barked. She would have liked to go out on the sled with the dogs. She would when the doctor left.

He talked in low tones to Laneylika. Talk of heart murmers, weakness. Rest was his prescription. A quiet life.

Ranja felt the sickness in her heart. Winter would soon come and cure her. Winter, the source of hope, master of life. Whilst there was Winter, there would be an Eskimo to endure it.

Endurance and fear. A man needed fear. When an Eskimo forgot fear, he died. In the White Man's city there was no fear. That's why their eyes died. Forbidding Eskimos to hunt the bear took away his fear, his battle.

Twice the dream of geese. Yet it did not come a third time to Ranja. The end of her endurance was heralded, she must prepare for flight. She must not let Laneylika be weighed down by carrying her. She would accept the inevitable.

The aeroplane came when the dogs were pointing their noses high into the wind. They circled, they fretted a storm warning. The pilot laughed at the Eskimo warning, but left quickly – just in case.

"The White Man never listens to anyone but himself," nodded Ranja.

They welcomed Mary and the baby home. The baby was now a plump and unmistakable Eskimo, bearing no trace of Mary's ancestry.

Into the pleasure of the moment, again the harsh cycle of grief intruded. Laneylika held to his mother a likeness of Janu. Not the painted White Man's whore, but the face of a bewildered and frightened girl overwhelmed by fate. "She is dead."

"Life comes, life goes." A cycle. A time alone with Winter would heal Ranja's Spirit. Could it ease the pain of losses and separations, and the nameless incessant longings?

"But there is more, old mother," Mary adopted the familiar title, "see." She drew from the shadows beyond Ranja's failing sight, a child of four or five Springs. Half Eskimo, half unknown White Man. A child with no identity, but with Janu's face. The child was crying silently.

"We could not leave her begging in the streets with Father," Laneylika said, pushing the child towards her grandmother.

No, that would not be right. Ranja put her hand on the child's shoulder. A child learning the grief of loss so young, as she had.

"Now there are two Eskimo children for you to care for, old mother. We need your help," said Mary, looking anxiously towards her husband.

"And will this talk of walking into the Winter cease?" he asked sternly.

Ranja nodded. No sickness of words intruded. Laneylika had inherited much of Harunka's wisdom, he had planned skilfully. He had known she would not turn away the child.

The old ways and the new must blend. There were memories, experiences, to pass on to her grandchildren so that men like Harunka and her father had not lived in vain.

She pulled Janu's child towards her, and took the child's tears on her tongue and into herself.

Together they would sew Janu's likeness into the polar bear skin, they would watch the snow cry and flow as Summer came. They would hear the dogs whine of storms the wind whispered to them.

So many things they would share.

The wild geese had flown and it would be many Winters before the thrice dream was fulfilled – for hadn't Harunka's Spirit whispered that to her?

## Guy Russell

### *Britainland*

It's a real city night outside, orange sky, neon reflecting off the concrete, classic stuff. Out into those dimly-lit urban streets where the hulking masses of the houses – yeah, Kitchener Street, the Taj Mahal, past the gutted-out Kentucky Fried, Izzy stepping round the barricades and the dustbins and squeezing between the cars. And through it all the gentle rain is falling, lalala, sing it.

OK. Watch for the little razorkids round here, they try and toll you when you pass to fund their fucking boxnew LA Gear. Notice the 19th century church, the block of flats from the previous clearance, the 70s community centre, well, the remains of it, and Heseltine Park, with its new redbrick pavement harder to dismantle during the riots that will Never Happen Again and tree box aerosoled PUBLIC ENEMY, with single lonely dying tree. Quaint, huh? Private enterprise, with council help, has secret plans to develop this area into a ten-quid-a-kid touristland, sort of UrboDisney, ride the lifts, dodge the bottles, every other house a franchised dopeshop, and actors drafted in with shiny DMs and blond dreadwigs and plastic flick-knives to give a real sense of authenticity. But meantime it's still unspoilt for the discerning visitors I take round; I'm doing my bit for the cultural psychography of the inner cities and my customers can impress their friends with stories of the street. I tell them things like, casually, like, Oh, by the way, Izzy got beaten up in this area once 'cos of selling some slightly duff stuff on the wrong people. They took him behind that wall and hit him with two-foot staves. And my clients beg, Please, Mirry, show us the Real Britain, show us the underside, take us burgling! I have to schedule them these days 'cos there's so many, and I tell them, You mustn't overflood or you'll disturb the natural environment. They go for that, these rad-chic hepcats armed with their Media Studies degrees, all geared up for some genuine onscreen experience. There's a market for the tour; people want a Guide to reality, they don't want it raw and newly killed, and living fastframe with the rest cut out costs money. That's the reason crime is so hip, it makes life more like TV. Honestly, I can say it's a pleasant change to be going out with someone like you, someone sassed, someone – perhaps the only person – who really appreciates the Art in what I do. That's why I offered you the fifty percent discount. Drumming houses is my speciality and the favourite course I give. I pride myself on speed and lightness of touch and a certain cool effectiveness. I hope you get value for money.

So, breathing deeply, as we turn up Northcote Lane now almost house by house you can see how the neighbourhood gets gradually cleaner, neater and smarter. It takes the long mile of the hill, the plyboard giving way to glass, the weeds to lawns and the rubble to tarmac drives and by the time you're on the hilltop – You are in a Neighbourhood Watch Area, say the lampposts. This is Northcote Head where you can admire the trimmed hedges, the Audis in the driveways, the wrought iron gates and granny annexes. Through a few leafy avenues and on your left now is a typical example of an early 90s executive home. Notice the ordered garden, the tasteful curtains, the neo-Georgian porch. Don't miss the Milner alarm fixed above the door, the lights on in the lounge, the happy family out at Pizza Hut in Wake, we hope. Register this house: the owners are the enemy, involved in Animal Abuse, Communism, Freemasons, Progressive Rock, you name it, whatever makes your hate sharp. Izzy, he's into clastics, he just wants to biodegrade the world, but for me it's about aesthetic values; anything in poor taste I just want to recreate. I'll say nothing more on theory; performance is action, and the words can come later.

We'll look steady and assured as we go up the drive. Generally it's worth ringing the doorbell first to check that no one's in. If they are, ask them whether they want Jesus to come into their life, and then give it a week fallow. Otherwise if you disturb someone, although mostly they're more scared of you, you can get the odd psycho who's been watching too much pig TV and tries it on and then you're up shit creek, like, escalation.

OK, garage; her runabout is still there, his macho Jag has now gone. Over the wicker fence, always make entry at the rear where it's possible. Here's the extension, built out to widen the kitchen and making an L-shape of the back of the house. The line of poplars screens the view from the other side. Thus, we are not overlooked.

For the panes, we use a bit of sticky-back plastic; here's one I made earlier. It stops the glass spilling. Then I take out the broken section and lay it on the ground, there. Reach gently through the hole, and you find the twinflex that leads to the catch. If you turned it back now it would de-magnetise the relay and trigger the alarm, so you stick a pin in each wire and join them up to bypass it before you lever the lock. Got it? And then, well, you're in.

Inside now, you stay calm and concentrate. Be silent, fast, but don't panic. I sometimes do half a tab of Durophet about half an hour before to jack up my nerves. I find it gives me that edge and co-pilots me, you know what I'm saying? First I'll go through to the front door and put the chain on, in case anyone returns unexpectedly. Then I'll go back to the lounge and slide back the double-glazing and jib the wire again and open one of the windows. This is the emergency exit. If someone appears, we scat here and over the fence to next door and down their drive. All right? I always start with upstairs. That way as time passes you feel you're nearer the way out. Your heart'll be beating fast. Don't panic. Take a knife from the kitchen if it makes you feel safer. Laser Knife, it says. Made in Sheffield. I don't need to tell you you should be wearing gloves, trainers with light sole markings (squash are best, but let's not get designer about this, OK?), your clothes are dark and nondescript. Izzy has a woolly hat 'cos of his dayglo hair. I wear a parka although I sweat in it doing a centrally heated house like this. Most of all, just get into it and enjoy the buzz. Make it fun, create beauty, that's my motto. Here's a painting, appalling sub-Sisley via Snobsville Galleries. I don't lift it off, I just take out the knife and slash it so the canvas flops forward cresting like a wave. Great improvement!

Right, bratsrooms – a better bet than people think. They usually leave the whole of Christmas on the floor and these kind of kids have everything. The first one's smallish and crammed with heavy metal posters. I scoop a discman and a pile of Hypernintendo cartridges with their unit, some cash and a stack of CDs like Poison and Slayer and Maidenhead. On the door of the other bedroom there's a Holly Hobbie plaque saying Nicola. Over the bed there's a poster of three kittens playing together. Uh, when you open drawers, start at the bottom and you won't need to close them, OK? Just a small tip there. There's masses of Barbie gear, and My Little Pony and Sylvanian families. Everything's very cute cute. They're getting the kids well sexually stereotyped, anyway. Elephant money-box saying Big Saver. Yeah, she is.

The main bedroom, where the decor gets less honest, frills and roses everywhere, even the lampshades match. The jewellery is baubles; probably the rest is hidden away, and it's never worth grubbing for floorsafes. There's a couple of ten pound notes. I find some binoculars (Praktica 10 × 25), and a Pentax twin zoom. Most of the household contents is tack though maybe it's genuine tack.

In the ensuite bathroom when I see those colourcoded shampoos by the pink marbled his-and-hers sinks – well...

Down the stairs. It might seem like years, but don't panic. Back to the squitty lounge. Always check those mantelpiece pots, they can be little goldmines. See, the sheer ugliness, that's what amazes me about the houses of these made-it people. I mean it's one thing running some totally banal firm and conventionally avoiding your income tax and buying boring shares in British Rail, but then to spend your profits on fake chaise-longues and hint-of-peach wallpaper and fucking pseudo-pseud Ryman prints, I just think, No wonder the country's going to the dogs! There's a flat-screen TV with Nicam here, so big there's no way we could get it out unless we had a van. That sort of TV, people would kill for that down the estates where I was brought up. But I disconnect the streamlined black video recorder, a Bang & Olufsen – Steg'll love that, and it fills up the rest of the holdall. I use a brass candlestick to crack up the TV screen since we can't take it and then I slash the furniture gesturally in diagonals and leave the knife stuck upright in the upholstery. The kitchen: well I can see Izzy has already checked over the real oak veneer cabinets with integrated halogen cooker. Tripoli is the reference here, I think. I wade through the political mess. In the next room uh, tomato sauce installation decorating the wallpaper saying, basically, SCUM, not his best work, and as for number two on the shagpile, cliché city. Fucking piss artist, he's going, waving his penis. Yeah, cool fucker, I tell him, to keep him happy. Izzy picks up his holdall. I zip up mine. On the drive I get to know again how agoraphobics feel, the openness and the distance to the road and all that blank dark-orange sky.

All right...? I know some people think it's wrong to housebreak, and I respect their point of view, but forces drive us and what can we do? If I didn't do this, someone else would, and less well. Blame the system! In an ideal world, of course, I could use my skills legally. I'd get the recognition I deserve. I see myself on a Channel Five documentary about the effect of styleculture on juvenile crime, talking to Dick Hebdidge or Simon Frith, tracked on a job by a very clued-up camera, saying Art can be commoditized beyond the material, Simon, in a performance which foregrounds Reality, and then charges for it... But don't relax now, it's not over yet. Keep the big hood of your parka greying out your face. Be steady. Be assured. Once some people stopped me and Val and asked directions on the return while I had one of those suitcases with wheels in one hand and a sort of sound system in the other, elementary MDW. Val stood there and told them the way, cool as shit, BBC voice, suuper.

Now into the graveyard, a shortcut, and down towards the valley on the other side. The more distance you make, the more confident you get. The houses get smaller again as we descend till we come into Wake, which is a mixed-race ghetto becoming trash Bohemia. The night is cold and still wet but beginning to clear up. We'll dump stuff in Val and Mitt's cellar till tomorrow 'cos they're respectable. Val's got a job. She's in Unemployment Benefit which I guess is a lifelong career, but let's not go into that. Mitt's away. The house is up in that sloping street off the centre. Notice the Kungfu Centre, the video shop, the new old-fashioned streetlamps.

In the main room Izzy piles the stuff on the floor and it's an average haul, sixty in notes plus twenty in change. Steg gives you well below for what you take to him, the mean prick, but if he argues with a photogenic Bang & Olufsen I'm going to shop him to the Office of Fair Trading. I can just see him going But you cannot sheeft zem! His only life is money. I don't begrudge him, but we've all got to survive in this fucking city. We're out clubbing later, anyway, at The Lab, and everyone'll be down the Washington first. You can come if you want, it gets all that tension out of your system, you know what I mean? No extra cost, and you can meet Femmy, Winst, Sicko, artist jobseekers all of them. Winst works with vehicles, Femmy tutors chequecards, and Sicko is fucking brinnic with the incendiaries, unbelievable. He can make a timer out of six NAND gates and a feedback loop. Izzy's got people to see, of course. He's always on the move, making deals, grafting, getting on, that's what made this country what it is today, made us what we are. Did you enjoy the tour, anyway? All genuine, all real, no fantasyland that. And it's appreciated to have someone like you there. You wouldn't believe some of the nerds I get. I don't make much, as you can see. No one gets rich at this game. I do it virtually for Love, sweet person that I am.

While Izzy gets sorted, I go into the kitchen and get some beer from the fridge. I snap the ring off the can. In the lounge I put the TV on. It's Britainland – the badguys swerve from lane to lane, massive lorries keep appearing left and right, innocent motorists lose their No Claims – but you know the police are going to get them if not now, later. It's called morality. I turn the sound down, like I often do with the new shows so you don't get the homilies, and put the stereo on, and then I can watch the vehicles burning up to the thrash of the Dead Kennedys.

Izzy appears. He's gelled his hair back up. Dressed in black with his speedthinned body and pyroquiff he looks like a burnt match in its last flare. He comes up and sits on the side of the chair and puts his arm round me. He's all glowing and sweet-smelling.

What's this? he says.

Dead Kennedys.

The film, you twat.

Fuck off, you prick, I tell him. It's called How to become a New British macho tosser. You won't learn anything.

Wankers, goes Izzy to the TV, not hearing as usual. He tries to swig from my can. Get your own, I tell him.

I'm going to have a shower now. That sweat dries like it's the fear sticking and coating you, like evidence, and anyway The Lab, you know, it's one of those places the dogs sniff your armpits before you go in... Uh, sorry to talk money but yeah. Thanks, pleasure. I'll throw in some gear, as you've been so excellent. It's good quality, I use it myself, I can recommend it. At night you can take just so much reality and that's enough, you know what I mean? I got this mirror from Woolworths; see you later.

## Hilary Patel

*Cutting the Cord*

I'll know soon what my mother understood when I was born. Inside the truth is squirming. She's ripe and almost ready now.

Where shall I go, to understand the look that I will give to her – the one my mother gave to me?

From upstream, the voice of Mwepya rings resonantly as she frolics in her waterfall. Should I seek that place beside her shrine?

Over there's the baobab. Should I return to its hollow trunk?

Or should I go downstream to Chitambasa, where childhood lies buried with its unfocused dreams?

Far across, I see the Kundelungu Hills, heaving themselves above a languid purple haze. They beckon still, offering to eyes glazed with innocence a future beyond childhood; expanding horizons in a world beyond the village.

My face, mirrored in the river that waters Chitambasa, reflects illusions of that innocence. I see myself beside the river, playing with the other naked children on the banks, while *mayos* first wash pots and clothes. Bright patterned dresses and faded, torn ones, lie side by side. Coloured patchwork melds with glistening ebony under a golden, warming sun. Women flow past, the contents of their kitchens on their heads, babies swaddled in *kitengis* on their backs, small children clinging to their sides. Laughter ripples across the fun-filled water as fleshy folds of comfort embrace me in a world without corners.

I see a childhood bathed in sunshine, marred only by my mother's covert look I sometimes saw; that expression of emptiness reserved for me. Shackled emotion, slicing my soul, told me I didn't exist. Yet I was there, between my brothers, and I didn't understand. How old could I have been before I saw it first? How old before it bothered me? Growing up, but still too young to form the question. Too young till now.

Soon though I'll be that woman; the mother of a daughter. After sons I feel the difference. She's fighting even before she's born. They never did. So frantic for release, she doesn't know her brothers have been taken, nor that her father's dead; doesn't know we are alone.

The clouds are gathering, but it won't rain yet. There's only heat and heaviness, inside and out.

***

I remember innocence and I remember its severence in the belly of the baobab where I built a home. I knew that evil spirits lurked in corners, but the baobab was cornerless; round, like the huts of the village, and safe I thought.

Yet even then, horizons were receding, with taboos and commandments curtailing our lives.

At night, watching dying embers in the hearths outside, we listened to tales told to protect our heritage. We were taught of the spirits residing in nature and of the curses they could throw. We learnt of Nsonga who sometimes sent locusts, and of Makumba who caused the earth to tremble. And closest, most crucial, we learnt of Mwepya, spirit of the water.

A line of termite hills was the boundary. Beyond them we should not tread, lest we disturb her peace.

"Do not desecrate the waters where Mwepya lives. Treat her with respect and she'll not send misfortunes."

"Listen to the thunder of the waterfall, and remember always that Mwepya is endowed with all the power contained in that."

"Take her offerings so she'll not feel neglected and will not weep, to flood the village with her tears."

"But do not set foot in her abode, else she would feel abused and hence dry up. Her barrenness would cause our crops to wither."

And those contrived constraints, infused in me, were inflicted on the children which I made. In my tree house, a miniature mother, with babies fashioned from maize ears, or from soft clay scooped from the river's edge, I transferred the taboos of my elders. I brought corners, already developing in the world outside, into the baobab's womb.

Then one day, one doll, most precious, made from clay, broke.

"It's only a doll; we'll make you another," my mother consoled when, tormented with grief, I returned and related the outlines of tragedy.

She hugged me close, while I with-held the truth and didn't tell how it had happened.

I had told my child, "You must never pass the termite hills." But what if she did? What if I did? Yet I did not go – that time. Manipulating imagination, I sent my child instead. I, who had imposed the inherited rule, willed her to break it, then chided her for that. I scolded her with words I'd learnt, though she'd done nothing wrong.

"Mwepya will be angry and will send down curses on us all."

Sunken eyes, formed by a finger, stared sullenly.

"You should have made me differently."

Yet could I have done that? I held her close to comfort her and to express my sorrow at not having made her otherwise. She was as I had made her, and I clutched her closely till she broke.

I could not explain to my mother, the murder of my child.

So is that the place where you will be born – over there in my baobab home? No, not this time. This is no lifeless lump of clay inside and I will not bring her out in that tainted place where corners entered my world and where innocence was betrayed.

***

As penance for my crime, I myself would create the transgression which had not occurred, and suffer the consequences.

I walked to the place where villagers had left their offerings: a gourd of *munkoyo*, a dish of *meallie meal*, roasted sweet potatoes set out on a palm leaf. Though flies and ants feasted, Mwepya had touched none of these.

And walked on past.

The termite hills, their bleak outlines foreboding, warned me of trespass, but Mwepya's mesmeric voice coaxed me across the unadulterated ground to a place carved out by her, a little way up and behind the falls; hardly a cave, more a ledge protected from the torrent by an over-hanging rock. There Mwepya welcomed me, and there, to that haven once found, I often returned, to be alone with the water spirit soaking me in soothing thoughts. There I rejoiced in her freedom, if not my own. For the sweetness of childhood, already dissolving in the baobab, had further soured with the bitterness of puberty. Though our footsteps took us further from the village, the scope of our lives narrowed accordingly. Our role was set and we should mould ourselves to it.

Only Mwepya could expand those stealthily diminishing horizons as, listening to her voice lilting with the waters, I was allowed to enter a world away from ancient humanity concocting ordeals for young pubescent girls.

While the boys went out fishing, hunting even, with their fathers, custom dictated that we should seek out our own *kalamba* tree in a secret corner of the forest, and there prepare ourselves for marriage.

We should practise *kukuna* and so enlarge those special parts of our bodies.

We should cut small branches from our chosen *kalamba* tree, split them into pincers and with those distend the labia.

We should chew the bark and smear ourselves with juice to harden the flesh around those areas.

And we should use tender young *kalamba* leaves, rolled up, not for pleasure, but in preparation. These deeds were a duty we should perform in order to honour our future husbands.

I had no inclination to do any of those things.

Such silliness I thought.

While others scurried off, like nubile rats, between the tall *kasense* grass, instead of tending to my private matters, I made garlands of flame lilies and wild orchids and took them to Mwepya. She, who was little interested in *meallie meal* or sweept potatoes, grasped gleefully the small bouquets which I flung down to her.

Back in the village, my deeds of trespass went undetected. Not so my culpable negligence for inadequately performing those dreary *kukuna* rites.

The old crones called me in, and while calloused hands investigated, caustic tongues castigated. They mocked the smallness of my organs and my paltry concern for connubial obligations. No suitor would be found for me.

Spiteful sneers replaced childhood's billowing laughter across the water.

"Such wanton foolishness. What did you do instead?"

"I collected flowers from the forest."

Raucous ridicule over that. But I would halt their laughter.

"I collected flowers and took them to Mwepya."

Such sweet silence then, until they recovered, first called me a liar, then accepted the truth.

I was punished of course – beaten and ostracized. And no one held me tight. No one turned me to dust.

***

So I'll not take her to the baobab. Nor will I take her down to Chitambasa; will not return her to a rooted destiny.

I leave behind the baobab and the rituals in the bush. I wave goodbye to the Kundelungu Hills and the false hope they offered, but I take with me my mother's look.

New horizons beckon now. I'll touch them soon. First walk into forbidden territory, then take a step beyond.

Those desolate termite shells whisper not a hint of throbbing life inside. As this pulsating mite craves freedom from my body, so do those flying ants yearn for release from the dark cavities of their earthly prisons.

Imagine them, sensing that the rains are near, preparing their exits in a frenzy of rustling wings. Maybe even tonight they will burst out through the clefts they've carved. Clouding the night sky and masking the moon, they'll swarm away to die. Illuminated by the fires and lamps they'll court, they'll dance their crazed nuptial rites before collectively collapsing in squirming heaps.

In such a brief interlude, the bursting of passion before, their mating purpose satisfied, they will fall exhausted, their little bodies, so soon wingless, littering the ground, until the rains lash down to wash away the debris of shattered lives.

So tree spirits and rock spirits; guardians of the earth and plains, is it some all-encompassing plan which brings me here? Or merely destiny's caprice? I broke your taboos before and break them yet again as once more I cross over and, for the final time, enter the domain of Mwepya.

It's good you waited child, for now I'm ready for you too. Better to stay inside and not come out I'd thought, but you will born, so I can understand the look that I will give to you.

Through tangles of weeds and snares of thorn, the way becomes clear, the path leading away from all corners. This time I bring no flowers. Hope has melted into memories and it is only with memories and this life inside that I return.

Here my daughter will be born.

***

Duty, honour, respect; strange how, amongst all of those, happiness was never mentioned. Should I have expected that it might have been? But yes, I did, for it had been hinted by Mwepya.

And happiness did not elude me.

Despite my lack of manipulation and adherence to *kukuna* rituals; despite the threats and dire predictions, I found a husband. Ngosi found me, and for a while, the present moment fulfilling enough, we excluded the future.

With sublime selfishness we grasped precious moments of frenzied ecstacy. But in the town that could not last. Horizons soon dimmed in the square house with its corners, as the walls of the world encroached to crush our freedom.

I smile as I remember the wedding photograph askew on the wall. Such an absurd prelude to marriage. But they took that too, along with everything else when Ngosi died, because nothing was mine, they said.

So fast my rustling wings were severed.

Ngosi's wife: always that and never more, until a son was born. Becoming then BaMwadi: mother of Mwadi. My own name irrelevant and my identity obscured, not only by others, but by myself as well.

I scarcely remembered my mother's look when Mwadi was born; remembered it even less with the birth of the second and the third. For with sons came a rationale excluding questions. No training was necessary to prepare me for that role. How easily I moulded myself into the shape. How fluently was love transferred.

Ngosi, could we not have loved each other longer? Must love be so finely tuned to accommodate the mating purpose?

Yet there was so little space for even friendship to thrive in a life where emotions ossify into rituals of survival and where future becomes nothing more than a gruelling second snatched from the monotony. Memories of my mother's look were lost in the corners into which we crawled, while the mellow sun of childhood turned blood-red and shone on a void.

There was no friendly river blessed by Mwepya; only endless queues at querulous water taps, while the rancid stink of latrines replaced the pungent aroma of humic earth. With the last born swaddled in a *kitengi* on my back, and the second clinging to my side, I watched Mwadi playing out his childhood in the filth of the rubbish heaps.

I miss you my sons. I ache as I remember your laughter and your fun; your wails between grime-streaked tears. It pains to remember how I nurtured and cherished you, yet I must remember, less with pity for myself or you, than to premeditate how she would feel to have sons snatched.

They are gone forever.

And Ngosi is gone.

So too are the fights and squabbles when wages were spent on beer instead of food and shoes. Gone too are those rare times when we were friends.

Like the time I dealt with the girlfriend.

Little more than a prostitute picked up in the shabeens, I minded her less than the money squandered. I knew that reason wouldn't work. Men, after all, must have their girlfriends. Urban custom dictated that, and likewise decreed that wives should deal with the whores. That was expected of us. That's the African way and, without Mwepya there to guide me, my suffocating soul found comfort and convenience in those erstwhile depreciated ways.

From tenebrous crevices of thought, details of schemes devised by ancestors were probed and rooted out. I knew what I must do.

Ripping the stomach of the squawking chicken with my teeth, feeling the warmth of its blood in my mouth, I was doing only what must be done.

Watching the demented flapping of the wings as its life dripped into the calabash, I saw only a solution to the problem which I had. The act was as necessary as the stench when the entrails, curdled with potions, were returned to the belly, before the carcass of the bird, sewn up with papyrus, was swept across the ground around the house where the prostitute stayed.

The next time you saw here, she smelt so awful, you fled. And you, Ngosi, respected me for that. We were friends after that, for a while.

Friends too on the night you died. Friends until your headache; your terrible headache and the sleep from which you never woke.

"Broken vessels and a blood clot," said the doctor.

"Poison," cried the people of your tribe.

"Death by natural causes," declared the coroner.

"Witchcraft!" screamed your clan.

"The wife is guilty. See her weep with shame. She must suffer for the evil she has done."

"We always knew she would give trouble."

"We warned Ngosi but he would not listen."

"Driven to drinking by her wanton ways."

Abuse was not enough. The humbleness of my chattels notwithstanding, they would take them all.

They took my pots and the suitcase of clothes, the blankets and the mattress, saying, "Nothing is yours. It was Ngosi who gave you all these things, and since Ngosi was our son, his sons are also ours. We'll take them too."

But what of the unborn child? Careful consideration over that, until they judged the foetus valueless. With sex undefined it might even cost a dowry. Best to be rid of us both, they decided, though reasons were not so simply stated.

"That child she carries cannot be his. For that she killed Ngosi, lest he detect her infidelity. Adultress. Sorceress. See her writhing, demented with her crime and the curses she has thrown. Let her keep the impure child to remind her of her treachery."

So here I am, cast out like a badly conceived clay doll, though I did nothing wrong.

All I have left of the cornered life are this *kitengi* cloth I wear, Ngosi's seed inside, and thoughts of what I have to offer her.

The pains are strong. She's ready for her freedom now, and I will give her that.

Faster the pains come.

And stronger still.

And the more frenzied Mwepya's dance, her exuberance unabashed.

Through the membrane of memories I see a childhood and my mother's eyes.

A photograph of marriage.

A corner in a baobab.

A clay doll turned to dust.

A role in rooted destiny.

Suffocate the scream. Watch instead the primeval purity of the water.

Cast aside the pain and listen to the orchestration of the falls.

Push down and breathe.

My sons, are you happy?

Do they ever tell you of the love usurped?

Will you grow strong and have fine wives who will honour you?

And daughters too?

Will you remember me?

Bear down again.

And breathe again.

Ngosi, your daughter is being born.

Only to push once more.

***

My bloated belly bursts.

You give a tortured breath.

A chorus of insects chirs to a crescendo before your cries dissect their cadency.

Mwepya smiles between her serenade.

And now, with my strong teeth, I sever you from me.

Can you hear the bullfrogs telling us the cleansing rains are near, and the rasping of cicadas between the rustling leaves?

Do you hear the warbling of the songbirds in the cassia trees and the lonely cry of the fish eagle high above?

Can you feel the comforting caress of the sun and the welcome warmth of the rich red earth?

Do you tingle with the rainbow-shredded kisses Mwepya throws to you?

I'll hold you now and understand the look that I will give to you.

Filaments of myself fuse in a reflection that will never change.

My eyes in yours, my mother's and her mother's too, stretching backwards, and forwards to eternity, reflect the life I know; the one I've given you.

Should I snatch it back, or let it grow to see the hollowness of hope? Should I offer you a shroud of stoicism or in a numbing moment eclipse the pain with a velvet blanket of oblivion?

First, I'll give you a name. I'll call you memory, and christen you with tears which cannot mask the truth.

I've emptied my belly and cut the cord. Now I must clutch you close; smother you with love in fleshy folds; cut all corners from your world and set you free.

## Beverley Strauss

### *Time Exposures*

A metaphor for time: a flow of water, an ever-rolling stream. Analogues for photography: traces, imprints, spoor. But what is memory – the flow itself, or the traces it washes over? I'm no more certain now than I was forty years ago, when I hadn't asked myself the question.

I'm not even sure just when Gino Blake settled in Morecambe, or why he chose to. He looked as out of place as I felt then, an exotic presence in a place as homely and English as the egg and chips its seafront cafés served up. He had a cosmopolitan grace, a weary, sad cast to his expression even when smiling, and a set of gestures that seemed to forgive the world its perpetual hostility. His features were contoured with an Italian refinement; his English was fluent and unaccented. He never sought company any more than he repelled it. He was a curiosity rather than a mystery. He would tell his story, or parts of it, in dingy snugs – mainly to young people oppressed by the emptiness of the early 1950s, hungry for a glimpse of broader horizons than the spread of the bay. Gino had memories, and tales, of anti-fascist activism in Italy and Spain. He'd had a role in British intelligence during the war, useful to them because of his bilingualism and knowledge of Europe. And he was an artist. He appeared charismatic, "hip" almost, although he was really a figure from the past: a middle-aged man whose iconic status would soon be supplanted by the rebels of a new generation from America, not Europe.

I first met him one night soon after the death of George VI. I had no use for king and country, was glad that an eye defect had let me off national service, yet couldn't find an outlet for my discontent other than monotonous rows with my parents and drinking as much sudsy ale as an insurance clerk's wage would buy – not a greal deal. Pubs, dances, the cinema, desultory hanging-around – those were the limits. The desire and impossibility of sex, adolescent rituals and urgent, shapeless dreams cut me off from surroundings that all the same managed to weight me down. My mood that evening, as so often, was dismally matched to the lost, hopeless look of an out-of-season resort. A duffel coat protected me from the sharp sea wind, but I still felt the chill of unbelonging.

I was with the lads, names long washed away – two or three boys of my age who already knew Gino and had come to treat him familiarly, though never with actual disrespect. He was drinking brandy – wine was an unknown taste in Morecambe bars then – and talking iconoclastically about kings. They were no good, he explained, opportunists, all of them, who connived with dictatorships and despised the people they were meant to serve and protect. I was impressed by his candid contempt for royalty. Already there were loud, boring fanfares of press propaganda heralding a new Elizabethan era, and I instinctively warmed to someone of my parents' age who had no reverence for monarchy. His acid views turned off my companions, though, conservative despite their youthful poses of defiance. Well before closing time I was alone with Gino.

We discussed art. I had no skill as a painter, but I'd been given a secondhand Leica for my nineteenth and used to prowl the town and the neighbouring straggle at weekends taking *Picture Post*-style studies of ordinary life or moody, deserted corners in imitation of Atget. I thought of myself as visually expressive, counting the flaw in my sight as a perverse gift. Gino did paint, quite seriously, though he had no fine-art prejudice against photography, and he was committed to an ideal of the untrained, unrecognized artist that couldn't help appearing to me.

He said, "I don't exhibit at the smart galleries. That is bourgeois art, commercial art, you see, done for money and reputation. What is fame, after all? Mussolini was famous and powerful. You know how he ended? Strung up by his heels. No. I paint the life of the seashore and the streets. That is where you find the real artists. Art should reflect the everyday. It must be popular, not the domain of a few."

I did recall newspaper pictures of Mussolini's end; it was the word "bourgeois" that was new to me, but I quickly adopted it as an epithet for everything that cramped my style – home, the insurance company, the town that was thronged with herdlike, holidaying masses in summer and inert for the rest of the year. Gino embodied proof that you didn't have to turn into your parents as age caught up with you. I pursued his acquaintance. He never invited discipleship, but he welcomed my interest. We began to meet by arrangement and I got to know patches of his personal history as well as his views on art. He'd barely known his father, an agent for an English commercial concern in Milan, who'd vanished before World War I. His beloved Italian mother had died in a bombing raid during the next war. He had a wife and children, elsewhere in

England, from whom he'd parted years before. He talked of his wife with a tremor of stressful emotion and a deepening of his tragic stare.

"She took away my life," he said. "What I thought she felt for me, she didn't feel at all. When she told me so, when I knew she had betrayed me, I had nothing left except my art."

I was too innocent to grasp exactly what he meant, but his tone, the timbre of stoic suffering, added to the fascination he held for me. Eventually he invited me to his home, a flatlet in a two-storey terrace house just behind the promenade. He poured wine from a strawbound Chianti bottle, and I examined the pictures that were hung or stacked all around the meagre space. They were mainly of flowers, done in harsh, unsentimental colours that caught the light qualities of the north-western coast. I asked if he ever did portraits.

"I do, sometimes. But I have to live. My flower paintings are very popular."

Was that what he meant by popular? They weren't kitsch, but the subjects were conventional. It was a disappointment I didn't wish to admit, even to myself. I'd expected more dramatic creations that would confirm my belief in him as a romantic rebel. But I still liked to hear his opinions and I spent hours in his company, sharing ideas about painting and photography, till the spring, when I was offered a transfer to the Manchester branch.

I had to accept. It got me away from my parents, who found my habits annoying and disapproved of my friendship with Gino, and thrilled me with the prospect of an independent, big-city life. The work itself was equally dull, handling sheaves of claim forms in a grander office, but I had a bed-sitter on the Cheshire side with a bullfight poster and a lamp I had fashioned out of one of Gino's Chianti bottles. By the summer, I had a girlfriend, too, and drunk with freedom, I'd drifted out of touch with Gino. Janet and I attended concerts and exhibitions and French films that, for their day, were charged with a sexiness absent from the British and American cinema. We played our own erotic scenes, too, nervous with excited discovery on the bed under the bullfight poster. It was that time in every young person's life that preserves the flavour of uniqueness even when, retrospectively, you view it as a clichéd rite of passage.

Janet was a student, a Londoner, more sophisticated than I was, and though I sometimes found her boldness a touch alarming I was grateful that she had no time for coy games. We were a pair of weekend bohemians, finding a reprieve from workaday tedium, with no comprehension of a future. The grey fog of the fifties enveloped us as if it were an eternal state. We had to seize what pleasure we could, before we blended unidentifiably with the miasma. I arranged my leave – as the company called it – to coincide with my parents' annual trip to Devon, and Janet agreed to stay on and spend a week of the precious fortnight with me in Morecambe, nominally house-minding. It entailed a risky deception, and probable punishment, but the rewards seemed worth it. I explained to her what Morecambe was like, defensively overstating my sense of its awfulness. She said she didn't mind. I believed her. I was confident that we could laugh at it together, two superior beings. And I wanted her to meet Gino, who redeemed it.

Strangely, Janet didn't share my shamefaced derision for the Naples of the North. Perhaps because she was a social science student, or because she brought a fresh awareness to it, she enjoyed its air of humdrum gaiety. She appointed me her guide to its attractions. She responded like an appreciative child, not a southern sceptic, to Happy Mount's silly lights. She jollied me into sitting through a performance of *Ma's Bit o' Brass*, and she rebuffed my dismissive comments – I'd started reading T. S. Eliot – on the families who covered the grimy sands and splashed in the breakers. She bought sticks of rock and mailed them off to young relations. I still have a snapshot of her astride a beach donkey, her long pleated skirt hitched up, one hand brandishing an ice-cream. It's as meaningless now as an image from an old brochure. Her attitude puzzled me, but I was content to go along with it for the sake of our unsupervised intimacies at night. I was too involved with her to pick up old contacts, and it was half-way through the week before I was able to introduce her to Gino. At that, it was by chance.

We'd taken a stroll along the stone jetty, watching the hazy hills of Lakeland over the sparkling sea while anglers dangled their lazy lines. As we headed back for lunch I glimpsed Gino's bald scalp, browner than most but still reflecting the bright noon sun. He was standing in front of the Midland Hotel, a building I'd photographed a hundred times without ever capturing the formal elegance of its design. I grabbed Janet's hand, made introductions. Gino smiled his bleak smile. With solemn courtesy he asked us to have a drink with him at his flatlet.

There were fewer paintings there, so I took it he'd been selling well. Janet and I sat on a moquette couch while he opened a bottle. When he'd served us, he made polite enquiries about my new life, addressing me but looking at her. Then he asked her what she thought of Morecambe.

"Fine. It's nice to see people having fun."

"Yes. If you call it fun."

"They seem to be having a good time."

"Don't you find the English take their pleasures sadly?"

"I think it's up to them what they want."

"But they can only have what they're offered, isn't that so?"

"Most of these people work hard. They're entitled to a seaside break."

The dialogue was crashing its gears, and I wasn't sure why. Also, Gino was speaking with a pronounced Italian accent, slipping in superfluous vowel sounds. I'd never heard him do that before. I felt I should intervene, but couldn't find the words. As I'd imagined this occasion, talk would flow and bubble, but it was curt to the point of hostility. Janet hadn't touched her wine. I'd swallowed mine fast, and now my bladder ached. I excused myself and went down to the shared lavatory, only to find it occupied. I waited on the landing in anxious embarrassment till a man in a collarless shirt emerged, fastening his fly. When I returned to Gino's room the strained silence was unmistakable. I tried to revive the sociality by turning to the topic of painting, but it was a two-way discussion. Janet kept out of it, pointedly. When we left, using lunch as an excuse, Gino's goodbye was offhand, unlike him.

We walked back hardly communicating. Janet wanted to use the afternoon for reading, so I spent it processing film in the makeshift darkroom in the cellar. Even at tea-time I couldn't find a way to mention the failure of accord at Gino's: it would seem like criticising one or other of the persons closest to me. But Janet could.

"We'd better get this out of the way," she said. "He wants to do my portrait. That's what he said when you went to the bog."

"Really? That's a compliment. I was worried you two weren't getting on."

"Wait. That's not all. He wants me in the nude."

"I thought you said a portrait."

"That's right. He says he can't do flesh tones without seeing the whole body, that clothes give a false impression. So he wants me to strip off. Oh, he said I could take a chaperone along, you or a woman friend."

I was having a torrent of reactions, too many to face or even name. All of them left me feeling very alone. Janet calmly cut a triangular slice off her welsh rarebit and chewed it, awaiting a reply. Her composure struck me as unfair. I couldn't tell if she was being adult about it, or complaining, or blaming me. I asked "Are you going to?"

"Don't be wet. I've been to Italy. I know what they're like."

"He's only half-Italian."

"That's the half I've met. Look, I'm sorry if I've insulted your hero, but honestly – he's a dirty old man. He's a rotten painter, as well. You don't want me to, do you?"

She was right, but I couldn't say so. Gino had a right to my loyalty. Janet was used to metropolitan bright lights, foreign travel, a whole set of expanded possibilities that she took for granted. I wasn't half as worldly, or as educated. I owed Gino gratitude, for prising off the coffin lid and letting me breathe. Still, picturing Janet naked as he built up her likeness on canvas filled me with squirming, nauseous sensations. Rather than deal with them, I gave her a sulky answer and that led to a quarrel in which a medley of differences got aired. The false utopia of young love was breaking up.

That night we slept back to back, not touching. I was angry and couldn't sleep, and angrier at her because she could. She'd mentioned that Gino had told her she reminded him of his wife, a corny line she called it; to me it meant that he was trying to recreate, platonically, the affection he'd originally felt for a woman who had let him down. It seemed a small price for her to pay, especially as he hadn't sought to get her on her own. That was on one side. On the other was my possessiveness, the desire to keep Janet in an exclusive bond with me. Wretched and uneasy, I got up and masturbated in the bathroom. It didn't cure my worries, but it helped me sleep.

In any case Janet was adamant, so not only did we avoid Gino for the rest of the week but our own relations were fractious. Sex was sidelined, and the excursions tapered off. Janet withdrew into her studies. I mooned about, becoming more aware of our violation of local mores, which was indexed in the coolness of neighbours and a noticeable flurry of curtain swishing. My home territory was no longer magically coloured by Gino's spirit of subversion or Janet's unaffected interest and delight. Everything was going wrong. I was trying to sell my photos, looking for a way out of paper-pushing drudgery, but no magazine wanted to buy them. Little lay ahead for me except an infinite corridor of sameness. I was dragged back into the past, yet I'd forfeited the companionship of those I used to know. I spent one day cleaning out my room, throwing away Biggles books, table-football equipment, an entire accumulation of schoolboy junk. It barely helped.

When I said goodbye to Janet at the Midland Station our kiss was perfunctory. We mumbled stock phrases about seeing one another again in the autumn, without conviction. Her face at the window of the crowded compartment was half-whited out by reflected light, like a double exposure. I wandered off through the crowds of suitcase-toting arrivals, keen to wash away the sweetish chemical taste of her lipstick with alcohol.

For the next few days I got acquainted with the self-pitying consolations of solitary drinking, buying spirits and consuming them in my rearranged room, while Sinatra crooned on the Dansette: songs for stinging lovers. Finally it was too much like picking scabs. On the Thursday afternoon, the day before my parents were due back, I called on Gino. My thoughts had been hopelessly inward and circular. I needed to recover some thread of empathy.

As I rapped at his door I thought I heard his voice, again with the added Italian inflexions – the self-absorbed artist talking to himself, I supposed. Then it stopped.

I wasn't welcome. The door opened a few inches. I saw Gino's mild brown eyes, his smock and palette, nothing else beyond. There was an abrupt stillness. I'd appeared without invitation, interrupting his work.

He said, "Oh. Please. Not now."

"I'd like to talk."

"Yes. Yes. Of course. Come back another time." Anxiety and excitement blended in his voice. Apologetically, I excused myself. The door closed and I heard the talking resume. Wishing that I had an interest that would absorb all my concentration as painting did Gino's, anything to blank out my self-feeding misery, I headed for the nearest off-licence. The crowds on the promenade surged around me, deformed, as I saw them, by unthinking, animal happiness. How could Janet view them sympathetically, at the same time that she was snobbish about Gino's pictures and suspicious of his motives?

I had ugly visions of her coupling with smooth, self-confident men, and sought to erase them in boozy oblivion.

Inevitably, things got worse. The weekend was clouded by my parents' shocked and furious reaction to the empty whisky bottles and the neighbours' gloating reports of my immorality in their absence. When would I learn responsibility? What kind of home did Janet come from? When I snapped back at my father it was *don't be sarcastic with me, my lad.* The stale arguments deepened my depression, and the only way out of it was a premature return to Manchester. This time I left my room bare and Sinatra went with me.

I'd deserted Morecambe, but Morecambe refused to desert me. It soon came back via the front pages of national newspapers, which reported the finding of a 15-year-old girl's body in a Morecambe flat. Nude but for socks, she'd been raped and strangled, and most reports emphasised that the flat belonged to a foreigner and an artist, whereabouts unknown, facts which preconfirmed his guilt in the eyes of the great British public. The story ran on juicily for weeks, first while Gino was traced to a small frontier town in Spain, then during his extradition – his anti-Franco record counted against him there – and trial. His defence was that he had imagined, in a mental blackout, that the young model was his unfaithful wife: "automatism". It got him nowhere, except to the gallows. Janet wrote me a letter about the affair which I found rather smug. Somehow the insurance company learned of my association with Gino, and after a sticky interview with the manager I was asked to resign. I welcomed the dismissal as a blessing. My lace-curtain landlady also gave me notice. It seemed an apt time to move south.

The silver lining was that I at last found a market for my photos. I'd taken plenty of Gino, the case had been a much greater sensation than the Clayton murder just after the war, and even then the English press was greedy for graphic material. They paid me surprisingly well for my pictures of the Seaside Sadist, enough to give me an autonomous start, and I'd no compunction. Myself, I had no idea where the exact truth lay. The newspapers didn't care. My father and mother expressed a sanctimonious hope that the whole dreadful business had taught me a lesson – meaning, in essence, that it had brought me closer to God, or John Wesley, or the respectable values of the Chamber of Commerce. It had, but not that one. I discovered that a lucrative new career can be founded on a grim accident of pain and death, and that reality lies out of range of pictorial reproduction. Years later, my photojournalism from Vietnam was greatly admired, corpses and devastation by the ton; but there was no rush to publish the studious images I took of the grand French villa in Saigon that reminded me, thanks to the abstract geometry of its lines, of the Midland Hotel.

## Heather Leach

### *Saying Hello to the Birds*

I get on the bus and I'm thinking anything to take me out of this place, so I pay the money and sit looking through the window and it's all crap.

"Doesn't anybody notice?" I say to my Mam.

"Make the best of it, our Carol," she says. "There's no place like home."

Conversations never go far in our house. Our Jimmy's always got the telly on, so you can't get nothing out of him. The only time he takes any notice is when he acts, "get me a cup of tea", sticking his little finger up as if he was the queen.

So I get on buses. It passes the time. It costs you one pound twenty now from our stop to Piccadilly. That's as far as you can go, and as I said, it's bloody crap all the way.

He says to me, "Come on, we'll go down the housing." He says this while he's hopping round the floor in his Dad's bedroom. He's got one trouser leg off and he's trying to pull the other one over the top of his trainers. His cock's bobbing up and down like a dancing sausage, and I'm lying on the bed supposed to be waiting with my tongue hanging out instead of hoping Mam hasn't got bangers and mash for my tea again.

"You could do worse than Bazzer," says Mam, and I can tell she's thinking about my Dad and I have to agree with her there. "You're nineteen now," she says. "You can't just stop round here, hanging about and going on buses. That's no life for a young girl."

I knew it'd come to this, it was obvious really. Most of my mates, that I went to school with, they're already standing out on the front, proper women, arms folded, going on about other people's kids and the price of tomatoes.

"Well what else are you going to do?" says Mam, and I have to admit it's a good question.

I used to go about with Shirley a lot, before she got together with that bloke from Wythenshawe. We had a good laugh in them days, me and her on the tops of buses. We went miles on our school passes, sitting on the back seat smoking and singing. She's pregnant now and buses make her feel sick.

"Anyway Carol, we're not kids anymore," she says. "You can't just go riding about when you haven't got anywhere to go. What's the point?" She's always on at me about this club in Miles Platting.

Ladies' night where they have these fellers stripping off and hundreds of women queueing up outside, wetting their knickers. She's got another think coming if she thinks I'm going with her. No way.

Mam says, "You can't stop at home forever; everything has to change sometimes." As far as I can see, everything's always changing, but nothing seems to be any different. People keep coming and going, doing flits, and the houses get boarded up and new people move in. Then you get to know them and they're off again. And the buses, they keep changing as well, different numbers, different names on the front, but the places all look the same when you get there. We've lived on this estate, me, my Mam and our Jimmy, since my Dad finally went more over the top than normal, setting fire to the settee when my Mam was sleeping on it. We had to go into the homeless and I was glad to get shot of him after what he did. He took me to Blackpool lights once, when Mam was in hospital having our Jimmy. He put me on his shoulders and we went walking up and down, up and down. It was embarrassing being on my own with him. I couldn't think of anything to say. He's a bit of a piss artist, always has been. It only takes a couple of pints now to get him paralytic. Mum says he'll be on the Q.C. sherry next, swigging it on the pavement outside the off-licence. Last time I saw him was a couple of years ago in the Seven Stars up Ashton Old Road. I don't know what I went for really, but your Dad's your Dad. He says, "You'll be alright, our Carol." It doesn't give you a lot to go on.

They've put up a new bus stop. There's that Pakistani lady from the papershop, Mrs Siddiqui, waiting in it when I get there.

"Very nice, very nice," she says, trying it all out, sitting on the seat and touching the glass sides, "but the boys will break it, I think." There's this poem on the bus shelter and a picture of Shakespeare with long hair and a beard. We used to do poems at school. The teacher, Mrs Aspinall, (only the lads called her Mrs Asitall, because she'd got big boobs) used to read out poems. When she comes into the classroom, Nikko Tomlinson says, "Don't bother trying anything fancy Miss, because we've had everything. We've had films, tape recordings, making plays, sex talks, going on trips and we don't want to be arsed doing anything else."

She says "I won't do anything fancy then, I'll just read you some poetry." So we all go, "Oh God, bloody hell" and some of the lads put their heads on the tables, and Janice McCran switches her

Walkman up so everybody can hear the bass, and it sounds like a big machine thumping under the classroom floor. Mrs Aspinall was scared of us at first; you could see her hands shaking. She reads a poem, then she asks us what we think about it, and nobody says anything, well, nothing about the poem. There's plenty being said about how Nikko's had it off last night with Teresa Reece from the third year. I went out with him once. He didn't try anything, just got me a packet of chips and walked round the precinct for two hours talking about football. Mrs Aspinall never raised her voice, even with all that racket; she just carried on reading and reading.

Waiting at the bus stop, I get into studying the poem. I can't make most of it out. It starts, "Shall I compare thee to a summer's day?" and I keep staring and staring at it until I hear Mrs Siddiqui saying,

"You will be missing the bus, hurry, hurry," and she's on the step, and the bus driver's going on as well, "Take it or bloody leave it, girl, I haven't got all day." I sit on the seat which is supposed to be for the disabled. There's nowhere else and you feel a bit funny, with that notice, "Please leave this space for people with limited mobility," next to my left ear. Everywhere you look there's writing. On this bus there's a load of adverts. "Design Your Own Course at the Adult Education College", "Cinderella Comes To the Palace at Christmas", "Use the Bus and Save the Environment". You can't rest your eyes anywhere, without reading something. I learned to read dead quick when I was a little kid, but sometimes I wish I hadn't bothered, because it seems like all reading is good for is to give strangers free passage into your brain.

On that journey, it's all the same for miles, blocks of flats with grass in between, broken buildings and little rows of shops. Churches turned into warehouses and the warehouses up for sale. The shops aren't much cop, newsagents with cages over dirty windows, second hand washing machines on the pavements, bookies and video places, that's about it. But surprise, surprise, there's one of the new shelters at every bus stop with proper little roofs, glass sides and nice benches to sit on. All the way up the road, there's people on them seats looking pleased with themselves, and when they get on the bus it's all anybody talks about.

"Who's put them up?" this woman in a green scarf says to the driver.

"Nothing to do with me," he says. "I just drive. They don't tell me nothing."

A right charmer he is. You either seem to get that type, misery on toast, or the other kind, the one who keeps hold of your hand when you give him the money, and tries to get everybody singing. Either way it's a dead pain. Green scarf woman sits behind me and starts talking to the bloke next to her.

"It's about time they did something about them shelters. We've been stood in broken glass for months, and that graffiti it's disgusting. You should see what was wrote on the old shelter. Mind you they won't last, nothing lasts round here." That starts them all off about the youth, no discipline and it's the parents I blame, as if half of them didn't have kids themselves, wagging off school and nicking boilers out of empty houses. I look across at Mrs Siddiqui, but she's not daft enough to say anything about the boys here. Green scarf's still talking.

"Did you see what they've put on it," she says. "It's a bloody poem. Who thought of that daft idea? It's our money that goes on poems you know." I have a look at the next stop, and she's right. All the new shelters have got old Shakespeare on them, his funny little bald head floating and the words in lines underneath, black lines on white paper, no colours or anything. At first I thought it was different poems, but then I get the first couple of lines.

"Shall I compare thee to a summer's day?

Thou art more lovely..."

It's that one. They've put the same poem on them new bus shelters all the way up the Oldham Road.

It's raining outside. The bus smells of rubbery clothes, and the windows steam up. The windscreen wipers swish swish and it feels dead cosy in there. The voices are still droning away behind me, but I can't hear what they're saying anymore. I lean my face on the cold glass and make a hole in the steam with my fingers. From where I'm sitting I can get a good view of it, that poem, and I start trying to get the words in my head. Even though half of it's crap, I can't stop learning it. It gets to be a thing with me, like touching all the lamp posts on the way home. I used to do that when I was a little kid. I used to think if I touch all the lamp posts and say all the numbers right, when I get in there won't be any arguments going on, my Dad won't be pissed, and my Mam'll have chips for tea. I still do it sometimes coming back from the dole or Bazzer's. Stupid really.

By the time we get to the old Brewery, I'm up to this bit about the darling buds of May. You don't see many buds round here. Most of the plants are the kind the council puts in, hard leaves with sharp edges and all the rubbish gets stuck round them. Then the next line has something about Summer's lease being too short and you can say that again. The only way anybody knows it's summer round our way is when the Spinner's Arms puts a table and two chairs out on the pavement, when the ice-cream van's still ringing its bell after News at Ten and the Bacardi advert goes up on the railway bridge. Sitting on that seat, I keep hearing Bazzer's voice in my head. "What's the problem with us getting together?" he says. "You can't keep saying you don't know, Carol, you've got to have a reason." It's all he ever talks about these days, when he's not on about smashing the state or who's won the snooker. I do like him; he's got a bit more about him than a lot of the other lads. He says it'll change soon, people'll start burning the place down. I said, "What do you want to get a flat for if it's going to get burned down?" only he thinks I'm trying to be clever so he doesn't answer. My Mam's on his side. "She always was Miss Shilly-Shally, Bazzer, our Miss Fancy-Pants Carol. It's what's started her on this buses lark."

I manage to get another line in before we get to Piccadilly, "Sometime too hot the eye of heaven shines". I hate it when it's hot; you get everybody standing out on the pavement, sitting on their front steps, leaning over the balconies, and all the dust and the dog shit gets up your nose. The lads start driving round the estate like maniacs, burning the tyres and the police chase after them, so it's like a race track. You'd think it'd be better in the summer, but it isn't. The blue sky makes it look worse and you can't go anywhere, but you can't stop in either. You sit on the maisonette steps and you see planes going over, little silver tubes floating high up. They don't make a sound until they've gone past, as if they were trying to get away with it. Watching them planes makes you feel as if you're living at the bottom of a dirty big pit. The men come and spray the pavement to kill off the weeds, and they mow the bits of grass round the edges and afterwards there's hundreds of daisies lying there with their heads cut off. I like it when it's raining, when you can't see far, when the cloud comes down low so that it all looks the same, and you don't have to worry about anything different.

In Piccadilly there's that same poem at each stop. It looks a bit stupid really, them white posters everywhere, but most people aren't taking any notice. It's stopped raining so I go and sit in the gardens for a bit. There's an old feller asleep on one of the seats, and a woman with piles of carrier bags, but they don't bother me. I can hear Bazzer talking in my head again.

"There's loads of nutters about you know. I don't like you going to them places on your own."

I'd like to talk to the woman with the bags, I'd like to ask her where she comes from, where she's going next, but everytime anybody goes near her she waves her arms and shouts, so I leave her alone. I sit there and say the poem, the bits of it I can remember, over in my head. It's like being on an island, buses and cars going round and round, and then this big drill starts where they're digging up the road, and birds fly up off the trees, hundreds of them in a black swarm, and then they come down again rattling and chattering nearly as loud as the drill. Nobody seems to be taking any notice of the birds either, but then I catch sight of the carrier bag woman and she's looking at them with a little bit of a smile on her face, as if she knew them, as if they were old friends who'd just dropped in for a nice cup of tea.

It starts pissing down hard again so I set off back to the bus. My Mam says,

"This is what I can't understand about it, Carol, you don't do anything when you get there, you just turn round and come back. I wouldn't mind if you were doing something useful. I think you're going a bit soft, girl. They'll be having you in the Psychiatric next." Me and Shirley used to think it was dead good in Town. We went in all the shops and in the Arndale – that's where she met that Wythenshawe lad, sitting near the fountains. I used to think there was something there I wanted and couldn't have. Bazzer says,

"All that bloody stuff, all them videos and music centres, it's ours as much as theirs."

He and my Mam go up regular and come back with a load of gear, pockets full of it, whatever they can nick. Me and Shirley used to do it as well, but I can't be bothered now. I think my Mam might be right. I'm going to end up like that carrier bag woman if I'm not careful, sitting on benches and saying hello to the birds.

On the way back there's more people standing in the bus shelters, some of them not even waiting for buses, just keeping out of the rain. I want to shout at them, "Get out of the bloody way, I can't see the poem." By the time we get to the old chimney, I'm nearly at the end. "Nor shall death brag.." it says. I used to think about dying a lot. You look at old people and it suddenly dawns on you that they haven't always been like that. I started my periods and that was it. "You can't go running about the streets now, you know," my Mam said, and I had to stay in, or lean on walls like the older girls, or sit on the maisonette steps talking and talking. Nobody ever used to say anything about death though, but I thought about it all the time. I'd wake up in the night and lie there wondering what it was I'd forgotten. Then I'd remember and I could never go back to sleep again after that.

When I get off at our stop, I sit on the seat reading the poem over and over. I can't make out what the last part means, "so long lives this and this gives life to thee."

I used to get really pissed off with some of them poems that Mrs Aspinall read. "Why don't they write them in bloody English, Miss?" She says, "You'll have to write your own, Carol," and Nikko Booth starts singing, "Carol is a barrel," so I give him, "Nikko is a dicko," and then the bell goes so that's the end of that. It starts going dark in the shelter and the poem gets dim, but it's in my head now, so it doesn't matter. Somebody's written Man United in black felt tip on the glass so while I'm sitting there I scratch "CAROL" in little letters on the back of the seat with my nail file. Lots of buses come and go, but I still stop there, until that Mrs Siddiqui gets off.

"What is the matter? Here you are again," she says and she can see I've been crying my bloody eyes out, and I feel a right fool skriking like a kid in a bus shelter.

I told Bazzer I wasn't going down the housing. He was dead pissed off. He wants to get away from his Dad and who can blame him, but I says, "I'm not going so you can forget it." My Mam says I'll have to find somewhere else anyway. "You're too big to stop at home at your age." I think she's thinking about shacking up with the bloke who catches ping pong balls at the bingo, and he's got two kids of his own so I can see the way her mind's bending.

Next week when I get my dole money I'm going on a bus that goes the other way. I'll see if there's anything different up there. It looks the same, but you never know. They've got adverts in the bus shelters now. At our stop there's one for Lean Cuisine Dinners where the poem used to be.

"They won't be putting any more poems in," says one of the drivers. "They only had one set, that Shakespeare feller, and they only put him in until they'd got enough adverts." He says this while the bus's going along, and all the people sitting on the bottom deck who can hear him have a good laugh at the idea of anybody giving a bugger.

## David Stephenson

### *Stepping Off*

I christen them, I marry them, I bury them. Occasionally – and this is hardest on my faith – I watch them die, often in pain, rarely with ease.

How reluctantly we go to God.

There wasn't much left of the old man. What the surgeons had neglected to hack away had withered to the point of no return, scarcely disturbing the thin green cover of the hospital bed. Everyone was amazed he'd lasted this long.

He was fed by tubes. A sign above the bed insisted NIL BY MOUTH, so I helped myself to a handful of his grapes. They were bitter. I felt my mouth being drawn into a grimace. The top of his locker – apart from the grapes, and a rather mocking calvary of Get Well Soon cards – had an expectant bareness about it. The Great Cleaner is coming, it seemed to suggest. Won't be long now.

"The wife send you, did she?"

His voice came as a surprise: much stronger than I'd expected, and edged with the barest hint of laughter. Even the film of pain that clouded his eyes could not entirely hide his inner amusement. The joke, I suspected, was on me.

"She thought you might like someone to talk to," I said, acutely conscious of my clerical collar. The medium was the message.

"Women!" he snorted, then closed his eyes and fell asleep.

Why did I stay? Why did I continue to sit there through that long, hot, drowsy afternoon?

Partly, I suppose, it was for his wife, Ethel's sake. For many years, forever it seemed – long before I came to this parish – she had arranged the flowers in the Morning Chapel, pottering about in the same coat and hat she wore for Sunday services. Him, I knew only indirectly, mainly for the condescension of his gestures as he ushered me into her presence whenever I called on Church business. Ethel's was the sort of faith that comforts, the sort that is a good fifty years out of date. His, I surmised, was non-existent.

"Tom's a good man," she often insisted, though I would never raise the subject myself. "And deep down he believes, I know he does."

On one occasion she told me: "His father was a lay preacher, you know. He must believe, mustn't he?"

How I envied her that imperative.

And so I sat watch while he slept his life away, occasionally shifting my chair to avoid the glare of the sun. A pretty nurse came and took his pulse, holding his wrist like a delicate flower stem, painstakingly entering the result on a chart. Her professional smile was brief and perfunctory, and I was aware that, for her too, I symbolised the very thing that could never be defeated, that made a mockery of all her skill, all her compassion. I was – am – God's vulture, waiting for the pickings. I was pleased to see the back of her.

"Still here?" said the voice from the bed. "I'd have thought you'd have better things to do."

Although my calling had accustomed me to a wide range of human responses in the face of death, it had never quite prepared me for that sort of conversational grumbling. It lacked gravity, as if this was a day like any other.

"Only a Parish Council meeting," I said. "They're usually very dull affairs. On the whole, I think I'd rather be here."

"On the whole, I'd rather be in Philadelphia," he said.

I grew alarmed at the coughing and wheezing that punctuated this statement. I was about to reach for the buzzer when it struck me that it was only what remained of his laugh.

"That's what W C Fields had them carve on his headstone," he said, when he'd recovered. "Do you know what he said when someone asked why he never drank water?"

"No."

"Fish fuck in it." Again, that hacking ruin of a laugh. "Fish fuck in it!" he repeated gleefully.

There is something terribly poignant about death-bed bravado. These days it makes me think of that Chinese student facing up to the tank.

"We don't have to talk," I said. "I'll go, if that's what you'd prefer."

"I liked Mae West, too," he went on, as if he hadn't heard me. "And Gary Cooper, James Stewart, Bette Davis. The new ones can't hold a candle to the likes of them. We did all our courting in the back row of the Gaumont, and in her mam's front parlour when the family was out. Bombed flat in '41, it was. Canary came through it alright, though. Is she here yet?"

It took me a few seconds to realise that the question was directed at me, and a few seconds more to understand that he was referring to his wife.

"She's resting," I said. "She'll be in later."

He seemed to have problems with this piece of information, repeating the word 'resting' over and over till it lost all meaning. Finally, something must have clicked.

"Oh, aye," he said. "She'll need to put the children down first."

I couldn't help smiling. His son was fifty-two and worked in London. His daughter had died in a car crash two years before, at the age of forty-eight. My smile faded by degrees, leaving my face feeling stiff and unnatural.

"The doctor says another one would kill her. You'll tell her that, won't you, son? You'll make her see sense?" His agitation was as real as it must have been all those years ago, when the fear was fresh.

"I'll tell her," I promised.

He began to wheeze again. "She'll have it gift-wrapped or not at all."

I have never known whether to look on the final disintegration of memory as a blessing or a curse. A bit of both, I suppose, but it appears to be so arbitrary that it's impossible to ascribe a function to it. Certainly, I can see no place for it in God's plan, but then it's not for us to question God. The only trouble is that the love of God, which passeth all understanding, is sometimes indistinguishable from indifference.

The old man started to sing. "There is a green hill far away," he croaked, then forgot the words and hummed a few bars.

"Aye, and there was a small rocky one next to it," he said, breaking off from the tune when it became unrecognisable. "I used to play there as a kiddy. I was always the one who looked for new ways to climb it, routes no one else dared try." He shivered. "God, that sun's hot!"

His limbs twitched beneath the covers like a dreaming dog's; his bony fingers pawed at unyielding surfaces. He was back there, climbing the hill. Suddenly his body went rigid, hands bent into impossible claws, eyes bulging in terror.

I was certain then that his hour had finally come.

"What is it? Are you in pain? Shall I call the nurse?"

"Ah've lost me footing," he whispered. It was a small boy's voice, the accent almost too thick for me to penetrate. "Ah'm hanging on by me fingertips. There's nowt below wuh but boulders and scree. What'll ah dee, mister? What'll ah dee?"

"Isn't there anybody there who can help you?" I asked. "Someone you can call out to?"

"There's nobody, man! Me mam and dad are working on the allotment. Arl me friends are playing footy. There's nobody here!"

I swallowed, and said: "There's always God." It was cheating in a way, but I couldn't bear to see him in more pain, a different pain. "Call on Him, and He will hear you."

But I was too late. The child had fled back to wherever the child came from, and the old eyes were once again laughing up at me.

"You lot never give up, do you? Tell me, how fast can an angel fly?"

I laughed, partly from relief but mostly at the incongruity of the question. At least it was more original than the old theological poser about how many could balance on the head of a pin. "How fast do you want an angel to fly?"

"No," he said, "that's a real question for you. How fast can an angel fly?"

"I don't know. As fast as it needs to, I suppose. Why do you ask?"

"My father always told me to put my trust in God and His angels." He shook his head, almost sorrowfully. "Could have killed me, could that."

I waited for him to explain, but he seemed to have lost the thread.

"Funny how some things stick, isn't it? Must be over sixty years, now." He frowned. "It's the same with milk. I never drank the stuff from being a lad but now I'm greedy for it, son, greedy for it. I remember when..."

He was drifting away again, dipping at random into the rockpools of his memory.

"The hill," I reminded him, "What happened on the hill?" It suddenly seemed important that I find out.

"Hill? Oh, that hill! I thought it was easy, see. All I had to do was let go, and God would send His angel to catch me before I hit the ground. Now! I kept thinking, Do it now! But my fingers just wouldn't let go. I remember looking down to see if the angel was there yet."

Time stretched. A porter came through the ward, singing. The pretty nurse paused at the foot of the bed then went away again.

"There was a narrow ledge, see, just next to my foot," he said eventually. "I hadn't seen it first time. Panic, I suppose. Two minutes later I was at the top. Very fine grass up there, it was, like velvet."

"Perhaps the angel guided your foot," I suggested. "Or in some way caused you to look down?"

The wheezing laugh was prolonged and painful. "Or perhaps the bugger got caught in the rush hour coming through Limbo! No, son, there never was an angel. Just me and that bloody rock, like always."

"It's a question of faith," I said. "You have to have faith."

"Aye, faith," he said. "That's what it is, isn't it? Stepping off the rock face and hoping someone will catch you. I could never bring myself to do that."

"It's nothing to do with hope," I said, "more a matter of knowing. That's what true belief is all about."

"True belief?" He looked smug. "That's a contradiction in terms, vicar."

And it struck me then that, though people may have all sorts of reasons for stepping off the rock face, faith is rarely one of them. Only a very young child – one too young to articulate what it feels – can have that sort of belief in goodness. The rest of us just cling on.

"Is she here yet?" he asked.

The sun was low on the horizon. I looked at my watch. "Soon," I said. "She'll be along as soon as she's rested."

"I'm glad she's not here," he said.

Then he closed his eyes, and stepped off the rock face, and an angel caught him.

I think.

## Mary Sara

### *Crossing the Wood*

The wood where she first felt fear was not so much green as pink in her memory. A mat of russet pink larch needles silenced all footsteps; it was a good place to find pink campions after the bluebells and that day there had been serene spikes of fox gloves at its edge. Through it lay a short cut and although she had not been told not to go that way she knew she was supposed to go round by the fields and then under the fence, and so into their neighbours' yard and to the farm house. Every other time she had done as she had been told. There were so many don'ts and ought nots punctuating her life like warning signs, all pointing away from both pleasure and danger. She did not know, at eight years old, where the rules came from, only that to obey them, even anticipate them whenever possible, kept her safely hobbled like the gypsies' piebald ponies.

Her dark pig tails bounced gently on her shoulder blades, their check ribbons silkily grazing the cotton of her dress. When her hair was newly washed, as today, they were knotted and bowed on top of tightly wound rubber bands to stop them sliding off the smooth twisted bundles they confined. She was never allowed to wear her hair loose, not that she had ever asked for it to be so, she knew better than to ask for anything that was not possible or approved. She seemed so often in the wrong, without knowing why, that she believed the whole world knew better than she what was best for her, what was right.

It had been an uncharacteristic deviation, that sudden turn off the path across the field, to follow the hedge and enter the wood, bending under the barbed wire and scrambling across the almost dry ditch before stepping into the trees. After the bright July sunshine her eyes were confused for a few moments by the comparative darkness. The copse was a plantation and the trees stood in rows on long ridges that crossed her route to the other side. After trotting up and down them with scurrying little runs for a while, she paused to quieten her panting and excited pulse. She flopped down on to the soft piles of old needles and leant back against the rough trunk of a larch.

Wrapping freckled arms round bare knees drawn up to her chest, she gazed upwards to where green frond-like branches waved in the blue sky. A fluctuating dapple of sunshine fell on to the ground beside her and she put out a hand to see if it was warm or somehow cooled by what it had travelled through. It was neither warm nor cool but flickered on her skin, gilding her fingers where it fell. She stayed there, quite still, passing her hand in and out of the tiny pools of light, absorbed in her game, for several minutes. Each time she thought that she ought to move on she remained, as if rooted like the tree.

When she thought of herself moving out of the wood she saw her body emerging on to the grass verge and skipping down the dusty lane. She pictured the huge walnut tree in front of the house that Mrs Randles made her pickled walnuts from every year. They rarely ate them fresh except for the ones she sometimes picked out of the grass and carried away, to peel, green and bitter-smelling and prise open with a kitchen knife. Her mind took her into the yard, up the steps and into the cool whitewashed outer kitchen. She saw herself lifting the latch on the inner door and entering the house place where the old black-leaded range would have its usual complement of brass candlesticks, in pairs like sets of twins, at either end of the mantelpiece. The fire would be glowing, adding an artificial heat to the stuffy room, pungent now with the smells of newly baked cakes and pastry. It was Saturday morning and she was going to help Mrs Randles with her baking.

Helping meant scraping the mixing bowl with her fingers and sucking from them the grainy mixture of butter, sugar, flour and eggs. It involved putting all the ingredients away. Eggs and butter to the larder, flour and sugar to the cupboards of the dresser and the brass scales and their pyramid of dark brown weights to the pantry shelf. She was used to such chores at home, and more. Everyone had their jobs to do, it was rarely possible to do nothing – and if she did, she tried to make sure she was out of sight. A favourite place was the top of the stairs, preferably with a book – so that she could pretend to be either just on her way to or from the bathroom and not merely day-dreaming. Her mother must have understood that helping in another household made her feel valued not used, though years later she often wondered whether her mother had felt jealous of Mrs Randles – to have had her help and her company so willingly given. True, the old lady demanded something else – an eager listener, and her mother did not, until she was in her teens when the burden of listening often became too great.

Mrs Randles talked of her middle-aged, bachelor son, working outside somewhere. It was 'Our Frank' this and 'Our Frank' that, though there was no husband or father. She talked of who she had seen on her weekly trip to the village, what they had said to her, what she had said to them. After they had cleared the oilcloth laid over the big table in the centre of the room it had to be swept of debris and washed. The girl enjoyed doing this. There was a satisfying order and logic to the operation she liked. First she swept all the sugary, floury scatterings into a pile and over the edge of the table into one of the big smeary mixing bowls. Then the old woman shuffled through from the scullery where she had been washing up with an enamel bowl of soapy water, set it down on the cloth and let her begin. She was too small to reach right across the table so had to stretch on tiptoe from all sides. When it was done, the dishcloth was rinsed and wrung before a last shiny wipe, and then hung out on the peg outside the back door.

All this she was doing in her mind's eye when she saw him, and was suddenly, deeply, coldly afraid. About a dozen yards from where she was sitting there was a small flat clearing, lit as if from a spotlight above by full sunlight. Her view of it had been partly obscured by a low mound of brambles pierced by foxgloves. The stomach-churning emotion of real fear was new to her. She was used to being nervous, scared really – of a telling off, being found out in some minor infringement, of a harsh word, but this was so different, so physical, that she did not at first know what it was. Her skin tightened and she thought it would wrinkle, and flicker of its own accord. Like a horse could brush off a fly by twitching its loose coat she felt she ought to be able to cast off her terror.

Had he been there all the time? If she had not stopped would she have stumbled into that circle of light – and him? What would have happened then? Had he arrived while she had been tree top gazing? If he had he must have walked very quietly, how could she not have heard him? What else had she not heard or seen? More importantly, who had also seen her? The tight system of regulation she lived under had rendered her pathetically self-conscious. Twenty years later she told her own children that others were not nearly so interested in watching them as getting on with their own lives, but she only half believed it. She observed people so intently herself, for all the unconscious indicators of who and what they really were, she was convinced others did too.

For the same reason she told them that a bee or spider was more frightened of them than they were of it. As a child she panicked at the sight of a wasp or bee, flapping her arms so that, inevitably, she was stung. Then would come hot poultices of Kaolin smeared on lint and swathes of crepe bandages smelling of the doctor's surgery. Calming their fears gave her freedom from her own.

After the initial terror, her next reaction, of guilt – at the possibility that the man had seen her, was born out of her experience that all adults could find a reason for you not being where you were. If you were in your bedroom you should be in the kitchen, if in the garden – the house, the fields – the village, the class room – the playground. The wood – Mrs Randles's kitchen – this time it really was all her own fault and confirmed for decades to come the obedient passivity that it would take an emotional earthquake to remove.

Her breath seemed to have stopped and her body turned into something as barely alive as the tree trunk she leant against. She could not understand what the man was doing. She could see that he was crouching, unmoving, a hand extended, head pointing towards the edge of the clearing to her right. Whilst she wanted to get up and run she dare not. Though she wanted desperately not to be there she could not move an inch.

He looked like a collapsed scarecrow. A stained and ancient gabardine, indeterminate in colour, was tied round his middle with a filthy length of binder twine and drooped on to the ground about him like wings, hiding his feet and legs apart from one cracked boot. At the clay coloured and crazed skin of his neck was a fragment of striped cloth that looked as if it might have been torn from the tail of one of her father's flannel working shirts. On the ground beside him was a knapsack, billy can and small bundle of something wrapped in newspaper. She could see the shape of his head modelled by a drooping and lifeless hat that was greasy with age. She was relieved that she could not see his face. If she could it would have meant he would have been able to see hers.

His outstretched hand was absolutely still and she wondered how he could hold it like that for so long without wavering. How long had he been there? Had he been there for minutes, hours or days? Had he been there before she had come into the wood or arrived after her? Following his arm and hand with her eyes she saw where they pointed, and at what. The equally immobile red mask of a fox in the undergrowth pointed back at the man like an arrow. If she ran now, both would see her.

Her fear was not stilled but increased by knowing what she was seeing. The man was a tramp and she saw now that he had been camping in the wood; a charred patch of earth and scattering of half burnt twigs showed where his fire had been. Tramps called at the house sometimes, asking for a bit of work and a bite to eat, or would be seen crossing the fields in search of mushrooms or following hedgerows picking blackberries. The few that came to the back door got a firm dismissal. If they persisted the big collie dogs would be permitted to rise and growl at the signal for which they waited.

Though her heart thundered and raced, time slowed to a trickle and a misting of sweat gathered on her upper lip as she sat on. The fox had moved towards the man so slowly and delicately that if the distance between them had not diminished she could not have said that any movement had taken place. Now she could see the animal's front legs and so saw the next hesitant step forward. It was as if the man was drawing the creature to him by force of will and the hypnotised fox could not help himself, resist as he might with all the instinct of his race. The next step came more quickly as if the closer he got the stronger the man's power over him became.

On the palm of the tramp's hand lay a torn crust of bread. Did foxes eat bread? She knew they ate rabbits, voles and beetles, that they massacred hens in hen runs and unlocked hen houses, biting off heads and leaving bloodied corpses. She had seen one once, setting off across the orchard carrying a fluttering bundle – supper for the cubs secreted in woods such as these. She had watched the corpses being cleared away and wheel-barrowed down to the midden and seen the terrified survivors clustered on rafters and apple tree branches like ship wrecked sailors on a raft.

The fox took the bread and disappeared. It happened so quickly she thought she had blinked and pictured it on closed lids. She caught the rancid smell of it as its brush flicked a low branch in passing; a smell like a mixture of old blood, dung and fur. Now what would happen?

The man still crouched, looking into the space where the fox had been. Now that what he, and she, had been waiting for had happened, her fear, momentarily suspended, came rushing back so strongly she thought he would be able to smell her. Her body hurt. Where her back leant against the tree she could feel sharp prickles of pain. Her knees were locked into a dull ache and she saw that her tightly clasped fingers had lost their blood and were bone white.

She knew that if, when, she moved, that pins and needles would follow. Pins and needles were a fact of life she hated almost as much as her brother's sometimes vicious tickling and teasing. She was an easy victim, quickly reduced to tears of frustration which would be followed by more torments. At that moment the idea of pins and needles helped her visualise a time when this moment would be over, a time she could identify as 'Afterwards'.

Afterwards she could not recall deciding to unwrap her arms, straighten her legs and stand up. When she thought about it, and she re-lived it often, she supposed her body did it by itself, following some imperative that she was not party to. When she remembered the incident it changed hardly at all, unlike other aspects of her childhood. As she grew up, other happenings, other feelings, took on a gloss of understanding, rejection or acceptance that seemed to alter the original in some subtle but profound way. The incident in the copse had the quality of indelible ink. It faded but stayed true.

Finding herself upright her eyes now fastened on the man's face. She felt unable to run away from him without permission. She needed him to acknowledge her presence before she could act, even though he was only a tramp. Her father and the other farmers talked of his sort with a mixture of contempt and worry. Unnamed tramps seen in the area were blamed for burnt out barns and blazing hayricks, missing eggs or tools lost from sheds. Gypsies too did all these things, she was told, but more as if what they did or did not do was natural not aberrant.

The hat turned on the reddened neck. His eyes did not so much see her as divine her as if she was like an easily readable page from head to toe. The slightest of nods, a twist of the face that might have been a smile, and she was off. Running back to the field, striding from ridge to ridge as though her legs were longer than before she had entered the wood; making a wind of her own blow the damp strands of hair from her forehead and dry the sweat on her face that tasted like tears; she scampered like a rabbit surprised in a vegetable patch.

She did not stop running until she was almost under the walnut tree. There she paused and dabbed spittle on a nettle sting on one leg and examined a scratch from a twig on her forearm. Hearing the noise of the breeze in the highest branches of the old tree it was as if normality had been switched back on. The whole thing in the wood, the man, the fox, her fear, seemed to have happened in utter, deafening silence. It reminded her of when the wireless, left turned on during a power cut, had suddenly startled her with uncalled for voices. The reassuring rustle of leaves and squeaking creak of old branches above her head brought her back, gratefully, into the known world.

The only thing she could never remember was his face, only that his eyes had seen and known her. She would never tell anybody what she had seen because she knew she would be told it, her fear, whatever it was, had been her fault. Mrs Randles was taking a last tray of jam tarts from the oven as she walked into the kitchen. The smell of hot jam made her feel safe for ever after.

## About the Authors

MARGARET LESSER lives in Altrincham. She has written a few short features for Radio 4 and a biography-in-letters of Mary Clarke, but has only recently discovered the great pleasure to be had from writing short stories – perhaps because of their almost musical organization, since she has always been as much a musician as a writer. She earns her living as a university lecturer.

SIMON GOTTS was born in Kent in 1957 and now lives near Chester. He studied English at Lancaster University, where he also took David Craig's Creative Writing option. He is a member of the Chester Writers' Workshop and hopes to have some work published in their forthcoming anthology.

ROBERT WATSON is Welsh, married with four children, and has lived in West Yorkshire since 1986, teaching Creative Writing on the BAH programme at Bretton Hall. He has written three novels, *Events Beyond the Heartlands* (Heinemann, 1980), *Rumours of Fulfilment* (Heinemann, 1982) and *Whilom* (Bloomsbury, 1990), which won the Welsh Arts Council Fiction Award.

PHILIP YOUNG, 35, is a journalist with a leading tabloid newspaper. He has published several short stories, including 'When Fascination Comes Around' in *Northern Stories Vol. 2* (Littlewood Arc, 1990), and a companion piece, 'Joyride' in *Panurge 15*. Extracts from his novel *Some Weird Sin* appeared in *Panurge 11*. He lives in Morpeth, Northumberland.

MOE SHERRARD-SMITH is a journalist and author, having edited magazines and a newspaper. She tutors in creative writing, both privately and for a leading correspondence school. Currently she has written an Air Museum Guide Book, a popular co-authored work called *Write A Successful Novel* and is working on a novel.

GUY RUSSELL was born in Chatham in 1965 but has lived in the North for the last five years. He is unemployed and in his spare time from jobseeking, is writing a novel about inner-city anarchos and ALF activists set in Sheffield. This is his first story to be published.

HILARY PATEL, married with two children, teaches at The Queen's School, Chester. Her articles, stories and poems have appeared in a wide variety of journals including *Passport 4* and *Sunk Island Review*. She has also won several short story competitions. Set in Zambia (where the author lived for many years), 'Cutting the Cord' was inspired by the plight of, and is hence dedicated to, Caroline Nchena.

BEVERLEY STRAUSS has lived in the north-west since 1991 after a prematurely terminated career as a college lecturer. He is now a freelance author and lecturer, also writing as 'Basil Ransome-Davies'. Other publications include a critical work on the American novelist John Dos Passos, articles, verse, parodies and short fiction. He is currently producing a third novel.

HEATHER LEACH lives in Manchester. She has been writing for a long time, but has only been sending work out since 1989. A few stories have won competitions. She worked for 16 years as a community worker. Now she is a writer, student and WEA tutor.

DAVID STEPHENSON has been Assistant Editor of *Iron* magazine since 1990. His first story collection was *Independence Day* (Iron Press, 1988) and he has subsequently had stories and poems published in a number of magazines and anthologies, including *Signals* (ed. Alan Ross, Constable, 1991). He is currently working on a first novel.

MARY SARA is a freelance writer on art and Art Critic for the *Yorkshire Post*. She has written *The Smooth Guide to the Galleries of Yorkshire* (Smith Settle, 1992) and contributed to books on artists. One of her stories was broadcast in 1989 and two others included in Yorkshire Art Circus's anthologies, *Yorkshire Mixture*.

## About the Editors

BERLIE DOHERTY lives in Sheffield and has been a full-time writer since 1983. She writes poetry, stories, and plays for radio, stage and television as well as novels for children and adults. Her novels have been translated into ten languages.

Her television dramatisation of her novel *White Peak Farm* won an award in the International Film and Television Festival in New York, and *Granny was a Buffer Girl* has won awards both in England and in America, including the Carnegie Medal.

Last year her first novel for adults, *Requiem*, was published and her new book for young adults, *Dear Nobody*, won her the Carnegie Medal for the second time.

STANLEY MIDDLETON, the English novelist, was born in Bulwell and still lives in Nottingham. He has published thirty-one novels and in 1974 shared the Booker Prize with Nadine Gordimer for his novel *Holiday*. His latest novel, *A Place to Stand*, appeared in May 1992.